SUPERB WRITING
TO FIRE THE IMAGINATION

June Oldham writes: 'I have always considered the story of Beowulf to be one of the best – for terror and courage, darkness and beauty, loyalty and fellowship, and dramatic, outlandish fights. Deciding to make a novel out of it, I chose to write it from the point of view of the young prince, Hrethric. Because I knew exactly how he felt: the man-monster Grendel had long threatened and stalked through my dreams.'

As well as her novels for children and teenagers, June Oldham writes books for adults, one of which, *Flames*, received a prize. She has held writing residences and does many workshops and readings.

Praise for *The Raven Waits*: 'frankly astonishing for the sheer force of June Oldham's imagination. The whole book is marvellous . . . it's a real shocker, but it is also first-rate literature.' *Yorkshire Review of Children's Books*

'. . . notable for superbly evoked landscape and crushing atmosphere of menace.' *The Guardian*

# THE RAVEN WAITS

## June Oldham

Hodder
Children's
Books

A division of Hodder Headline Limited

First published in 1979 by Abelard-Schuman Limited
This edition published 2001
by Hodder Children's Books
as part of Hodder Silver Series

A Catalogue record for this book is available from
the British Library

ISBN 0 340 79211 6

Typeset by Avon Dataset Ltd, Bidford-on-Avon, Warks

Printed and bound in Great Britain by
The Guernsey Press Co. Ltd, Channel Isles

Hodder Children's Books
a Division of Hodder Headline Limited
338 Euston Road
London NW1 3BH

For Alex,
my grandson

## List of main characters

| | |
|---|---|
| **Hrothgar** | King of the Scyldings |
| **Wealhtheow** | his Queen |
| **Hrethric** | |
| **Freawaru** | their children |
| **Hrothmund** | |
| **Aeschere** | Friend of Hrothgar and Counsellor in the Scylding court |
| **Hrothulf** | nephew of Hrothgar |
| **Unferth** | friend of Hrothulf and Counsellor in the Scylding court |
| **Angenga** | a scop or poet |
| **Beowulf** | a warrior of the Geats |

# ONE

His arms were stiff by his sides. His back was braced against the fur upon which he lay. There was no sound now. Even the whimpers of the children in the women's chambers, the sudden wail from the mother of Oslaf, had ceased. Yet no one slept. Hrethric knew that. All waited, their eyes open in the darkness; waiting. It was always so. When a thane stood alone in the deserted hall, his ears straining for the tread of the ravening visitor, the night was always like this. Hrethric could remember no night of waiting that had been different from any other. Even as a child, when he had crept beside his mother, he had received no comfort. Her arms round him had not been soft but rigid and hurtful; her body had not warmed his but was chill through her gown, and the tears which had seeped through his hair were sticky as the blood they knew would soon drip over the benches in the great hall.

The cold which he had once shared with his mother was now inching over him, bringing the frost to his fingers and the soles of his feet. Then it possessed him fully and his body shook. He clenched his teeth so that his servant should not hear the shameful sound, but there was no need. The servant in his straw at the end of the chamber, the prince under his furs, both knew that the other shook as the cold came and that nothing could prevent the shaking. The extra skins and the thick woven cloth of wool which Stuff always laid for him on the nights of waiting could never hold back

1

the cold. It came, and all must suffer it. It was easier to bear than what was to come. Hrethric dare not think how many times he had trembled in the grip of this ice.

Once, years before, he had gone with his sister to count the mounds. They had reached past thirty then, sickened by what had begun as a game, they ran back to the hall which stood clear and safe in the sun. The mounds were in memory of the men who had remained to defend their hall, veteran warriors who had boasted in their cups during the treacherous twilight, or sombre counsellors who faced the darkness out of duty to their king. There were fewer mounds now, less important and placed closer together, made for the young thanes inexperienced in battle, who had had the one occasion to try their skill.

Tonight it was Oslaf who stood alone in the great hall, Oslaf who had taught Hrethric to ride, Oslaf who was only two winters older than his prince. He had not told Hrethric what he intended. His decision was clear from the way he bore himself, proud but never smiling, for though he had chosen to be named among the brave he knew that he was doomed. But first he and Hrethric had done all the things they most enjoyed. They had fished in the best streams; they had hunted the stag; they had raced their horses on the firm sand under the cliffs. Each thing they did was done for the last time and only by the long, final look which Oslaf gave to each place did he betray his feelings.

The night remained silent. Nothing moved. But the cold began to change. Still freezing, it dripped moistly out of the blackness and all who waited knew that it was nearly time. Hrethric lay, his eyes open and fixed upon the dark above him which began to thicken and bear down upon him, stifling his breath. Until mist oozed between the folds of the night and Hrethric's breathing stopped.

Oslaf was in the centre of the gabled hall, facing the doors, knowing that his mound would contain no ashes. Hrethric's blood thumped. Oslaf was striding forward, his sword raised. Then at last sweat broke from Hrethric's skin; his breath returned on a long moan, as the sound for which they had all been waiting pierced through the walls.

The one high, thin scream.

# TWO

As soon as the darkness had begun to draw away and the iron corslet on the wall at his head took shape and glimmered, Hrethric called to his servant.

'It is time, Stuff.' There was no need to rouse him. No one slept after the waiting.

'I am going. I do not forget the queen's orders,' the man answered, adding querulously, 'and I should have done it in any case.' He pushed himself up from the straw and kicked it into a heap, angry that Hrethric had prompted him; but it was a gruesome task he was to perform and he had to will himself to do it.

'I am coming.'

With the door already swinging back, Stuff turned. 'No, my lord, it is not for you to see.'

'Oslaf was my companion! How can you understand that? It is necessary for me to go.' He had raised himself on an elbow and was shouting into the man's face.

'I understand, my lord.' Stuff's voice was quiet. 'Once the father of Oslaf was my master. When the dawn came after his night, I went to the great hall as he had bade me. It was I who wiped away the blood which lay in stagnant pools upon the benches; it was I who carried his sword, bright and unused, to his son Oslaf. I knew then that it would be only a matter of time before I should do the same for his son. On that morning I saw on Oslaf's face the vow to avenge his father.'

'He did it for his king.'

'That is true; but on that morning, Oslaf's vow was to his father,' he replied stubbornly. He stepped into the doorway, a tired figure bent against the pallid light. 'Kin must be avenged. Who, I ask myself, will think it necessary to avenge my old master's dead son?'

He had gone, leaving a question which Hrethric dare not answer. It echoed among the crossbeams of his roof and under the planks of his floor as he slid from his furs; it remained to taunt him as he lifted down the heavy corslet. He could not say, 'I will avenge Oslaf.' Even in the most secret recesses of his mind he could not frame the words. Because once an oath was made, there was no going back, and one night, when pushed by drunken courage or desperation to get it over, he too would stand between the long rows of tables in the hall and wait for the crack of his ribs in the monstrous hands and the spurt of his blood before the final darkness.

Without help, it was difficult to pull the corslet over his head. His fingers were trapped in the close mesh and the wristbands of his tunic were snagged by the armour's short sleeves. It had taken a smith many months to work it, hammering the glowing iron into perfect rings, threading each one upon the last, fixing it with a bronze rivet until the coat of mail was a mass of interlocking circles, the forged iron gleaming like silver and speckled with delicate bronze stars. A prince must have the best of armour. The smith had not boasted when he said that no dagger would pierce it, but the corslet had not been used. However odd it would appear, he had decided to wear it in honour of Oslaf, and he smiled wryly at the sentiment as he buckled his belt and short sword over his hips.

It was not yet day. Shadows still lurked between the chambers; they spread from the walls of the royal apartments and hung under the low eaves of the sloping thatch. They reached out to Hrethric as he ran down the paths and flung damp threads of spiders against his mail, as clammy as the mist. For the mist was still there. When he came to the front of the women's chambers and stepped through the garden, once full of blossoms but now untended and left to weeds, he could see other dwellings which fringed the space in the centre, and moisture smoked at the base of their wooden walls and trailed in wisps along the roofs. It was as if the horror of the night had left a memory of its breath.

Above him was the great hall and Hrethric climbed quickly towards it, making for the light which shone through one of the slits in the long wall. Nearing the crest of the low knoll, he looked across at the small huts and workshops grouped on the other side. They dripped dank and silent. Until the taper by which Stuff worked was extinguished, none of the servants or craftsmen would open his doors. At the wall he turned and walked down its length towards the end in which the high doorway was set, facing a wide avenue. Years before, skipping along that avenue with Freawaru, his sister, he had seen the spoor of the night visitor upon the paved surface. The avenue was his path. Hrethric could walk along it no more.

Before rounding the end of the building and pushing back the doors, Hrethric sensed a movement below him. In the mist, coiled in a shadowy alley between the chambers, something bulged, grew as if it fed upon the rank steam, stretched like an animal roused by the smell of flesh, reared, then divided into two horsemen. They cantered up the knoll. Hrothulf, his cousin, and the counsellor Unferth. Instinctively

Hrethric pressed his back against the wooden pillar.

'Why, Hrethric! Coming to view the sights! I see you are prepared,' his cousin said. Behind him a noise came from Unferth's throat, a sound without merriment which mocked the laughter it was meant to be.

'Good morning, my prince.' He showed himself, swinging his horse round Hrothulf's tall stallion. 'A dull winter's morning, is it not? Do we assume that you are wearing your corslet as a protection against the inclement weather? Or have you some particular reason for donning it today? What do you think, Hrothulf? Some special engagement, perhaps, for surely my memory serves me correctly and this is the first time the fellow has worn it.'

Hrethric blushed.

'You are confusing him, Unferth,' the other pretended a rebuke. 'One question at a time. I'll wager that he is practising, isn't that so, Hrethric? Getting the feel of it for when you join the geogoth, that intrepid band of young thanes?'

'You could be right. It won't be many winters now before he will be wanting to try his strength one night in the great hall.' Unferth cackled and this time the sound carried a hideous mirth.

That is what they want, Hrethric thought. If I died before my father, Hrothulf would inherit the kingdom. That way it would be easy for him; for Unferth, too, except that he would have to find some other cause for constant plotting.

'I am wearing it for Oslaf,' he answered, and watched their expressions change. More recklessly, he accused them, 'It is better for armour to be worn than to hang rusting on the wall.'

'Why, the young whelp!' one exclaimed. The horses were

7

pressed upon him; Hrothulf was bent forward, his hand raised, but before it came down, Unferth hissed, 'No!' As the other man wheeled round, Hrethric saw his mother ascending slowly towards them. Behind her, listless and with head bowed, the mother of Oslaf dragged her feet through the grass.

Hrothulf touched his horse and trotted to meet the queen. 'It is not right that you should rise early on such a morning,' he greeted her.

'That is a small thing to do when others sorrow.' She glanced quickly over her shoulder to Oslaf's mother. 'I weep with them. Their despair is mine; it pulls at my heart.'

'Your lids are red and there are shadows under your eyes after a night spent sleepless. Mourning spoils your beauty, Wealhtheow.' He climbed from his horse and as he stretched out to touch her, Hrethric felt Unferth stir at his side. Looking up, he saw a smirk pull at the counsellor's cheek.

Wealhtheow had stepped back. 'That is nothing. Perhaps tonight sleep will come.'

'It would come each night if you consented to my wishes. Each night, instead of tears and waking there would be feasting before pleasure and contented sleep. Why will you not listen, Wealhtheow? The time of the grey heads is over. The winters before you are many. We could make them joyful and free from care.'

'I long for such peace,' she answered carefully.

They were more than the length of a hall bench from him and Hrethric could not hear their whispered words but he understood from their postures that Hrothulf persuaded and that his mother responded with tired patience. While from his high saddle Unferth looked down at them like a chaperon satisfied with his charge.

'Do not long for it. We could make it come to pass,' Hrothulf urged. 'The grey heads can do nothing.'

'And what can you do though your head is not grey and your hand is steady? You offer no advice which is better than anything the king has tried. Last night he sat as he always does, dressed in his armour, his helmet and sword by his side, his hair bleached by the grief of these twelve winters. You had no comfort for him. He is your king and uncle. Now you rule with him and should be a support in his gathering years, but you can do nothing.'

Hrothulf's face tightened. The two regarded each other, the man tall as all the Scyldings, angry and resentful, the woman young for motherhood and royal cares but steady and unafraid. So she had looked when Hrothgar in the prime of valour had taken her for his queen.

'You should not speak to me thus,' the man said. 'There may come a time when . . .' He glanced at Hrethric and the words left unspoken were hinted in the smile which curved like the blade of a swinging sword.

'Hrethric!' she called quickly, but before he reached her they heard a cry from the mother of Oslaf and saw Stuff approaching them from the hall.

In one hand he carried a tangle of wet rags; in the other, a bucket. That was all.

'Is it done?' Hrothulf demanded.

Stuff nodded.

'Have you no tongue, old man?' he demanded again.

'I have a tongue, but no words, my lord,' Stuff answered, and his eyes resting upon Hrothulf were those of a man who saw other things.

'The place is ready. Aeschere has laid out a sword. Go, Stuff, with his mother. I will follow,' Wealhtheow said.

'That is not necessary,' Hrothulf objected. 'You stand by the empty grave of every young nobody who has thought he could do better than proven warriors. No other member of the court does as you do, Wealhtheow.'

'Therefore there is stronger reason that I should, though I do not think they stay away out of pride, as you suggest.'

'You are as resolute as any fighter in battle,' he admired, his irritation lessening. 'Come, take my horse, and I will attend with you. Then you must rest, my pale and lovely queen,' and as if he had never threatened, he lifted her gently into his saddle, took the reins and led her down the slope.

Hrethric should have followed. He knew he should join the sad line ahead of him, but he could not. The reason was in the bucket which Stuff carried, in the water stained a deep red. It was all that remained of Oslaf. He had been prepared for the sight. He had not been surprised at the revulsion which came with grief, but he had not expected another feeling. Relief. He had been relieved, relieved that it was Oslaf's blood, not his; almost glad. Dazed, repelled by this emotion, ashamed, he hesitated, running his fingers over the carving on the hall's thick doors. And gradually he knew that he was observed.

Still sitting on his horse, his eyes hidden by the shadow of the hall's overhanging thatch, Unferth kept watch. Above him, on the roof, summoned as always by a wind scented with blood, the raven sharpened its beak upon the horn-tipped gables. Hrethric turned and walked quickly away, away from the waiting Unferth, away from his black familiar hoping for carrion, away over the sodden grass, through the drenched tufts of the women's garden, past the lesser hall of his father's vigil, down the paths glazed with mud to his own chamber where a small sheaf hung among the rafters, tied to the wattle of hazel under the thatch. By shinning up one of the smooth centre posts, Hrethric reached a crossbeam, pulled himself on to it, straddled it, and slid towards the sheaf. He unfastened it carefully, looped the thong over his neck and dropped the sheaf gently on his back. The cluster of dried ears was sacred and must not be damaged on his climb down. Before leaving his chamber, he lifted his shield down from the wall. There was one thing he could do for Oslaf, a private requiem.

Taking a track on the perimeter of the court apartments, Hrethric left behind him the hall, steeped with the horrors of the night. Ahead of him, the patches of turned earth were gaining colour, warming to brown in the first light of the sun. The sight cheered him, for fields prepared for spring sowing promised that in a few months the night visitor's dark hours would shrink before the longer days. He did not see that the lines of the shallow furrows were crooked, that the headlands were slovenly with village rubbish: an unmended plough, discarded pelts, a heap of feathers and claws. A stranger's eye would have remarked this, but now no strangers came to the land of the Scyldings.

Flanked by a waste of barren scrub and a sluggish ditch, a village sprawled across his path. Fires were beginning to smoulder between the huts and, as they saw him, women rose from the smoke they coaxed and scurried into doorways, calling to one another and dragging children to their sides. One remained and wailed shrilly as he stepped over her, a scrawny brat with clotted hair and running nose. Hrethric wiped his own on his sleeve and made for the hut of the chief villager.

'Wihtgar,' he shouted, leaning against the hut's low roof.

The bracken over the wattle was thinning in patches and full of a scurf of insect shells, flakes of horn and the gnawed slivers of bone. Close to it, he recognized this neglect as he had not noticed the condition of the fields, and he saw that it was repeated in everything else. Through the door of the central longhouse he could see that the cattle in their stalls were thin and undergrown; further in, where most of the land churls slept, the floor was littered with chipped pots, heaps of dirty rags and soiled straw. Hanks of barley had spilled from their piles in the barn and lay damp and mouldering on the threshing floor. And this village supplied the needs of the court! For a moment Hrethric wondered how his cousin could desire such a kingdom. 'Let him have it,' he said to himself. 'Let him be responsible for it. It is nothing now, ugly and derelict. I don't want the bother of it,' but he knew that he lied.

Aloud, he shouted again, 'Wihtgar, come out! It is already morning. You should not lie so late.'

A grunt of a sow as it was pushed away, then Wihtgar's face peered up. Standing on the hollowed-out floor which gave height to the interior of the hut, the churl was lower than his prince outside. Hrethric smiled. Here his rank was acknowledged. There was no Unferth who spied and mocked.

'I have a pain in my belly, Prince Hrethric, son of Hrothgar,' the man whined. 'The corn in my woman's pot has fermented. It makes bad dough.'

'You have milk, have you not? Fetch me a bowl of it.'

Wihtgar scrambled out of the hut and called an order to his wife.

'This roof needs re-covering, Wihtgar. See that it is done.'

'The bracken and turf are wet. This is no time of year to

12

be cutting them for roofs. I am speaking the truth, my lord. Any land churl would answer the same,' thereby justifying laziness and also pointing out that Hrethric had no practical knowledge of the work.

Thus snubbed, Hrethric watched the woman drop hot stones into a vessel and heard the sharp hiss of singed milk. She brought some in a bowl and he drank, wincing at the dirt and grease congealed round the rim. A piglet snuffled at the door of Wihtgar's hut. Its long ears flapped in the dust; its narrow back quivered as it was driven by the instinct which told it to root.

'Give me that,' Hrethric said.

The man looked up, startled. 'What do you ask, my lord?'

'You know what I ask: that sucking boar-pup.'

'What would my lord do with that? It is poor and scraggy, less than a meal for a prince. It is not worthy.'

'I must have it. It is necessary that the blood of one should flow today.'

'My lord, we have little. The winter has been long.' The man was pleading now. 'The meat we salted after the month of blood is finished; the ears of the corn have mould; the birds we catch have little flesh. Please, my lord, do not take a small pig.'

'I must have it, Wihtgar.'

Beaten, the churl caught up the small animal and handed it to his prince. Its soft hooves were snared in the rings of his corslet as it struggled until at last he had it gripped under one arm. Leaving the man miserably scratching at the unkempt bracken of his roof, Hrethric walked out of the settlement, taking the track through the scrub towards the forest beyond.

When he came to the trees, some of the night's fear

13

returned. Oaks and beech were leafless, but their packed branches filtered the weak light so that it dropped cold and faded at Hrethric's feet. Roots ribbed the track; briars knotted over it; at times it was almost hidden by the forest's debris of fallen trees, flakes of pulp and the scum of damp leaves. The time had been when this way was clear, swept and strewn with sand from the faraway beach, trod by the priest and the king his father, his mother, thanes and Aeschere bearing the child Hrethric in his arms. Now he came alone, carrying a skinny piglet that had been born in the hovel of a churl. Oslaf deserved more.

A wide road, cleared for horses and waggons, cut through the forest. To his left it took a longer route than the track to the royal dwellings; to his right it dipped and wound towards the distant sea. Crossing this, Hrethric found the path again, and in a few minutes was pushing through the bushes which formed a natural screen for the glade he sought.

It was a strange place, simple and imposing, a secluded hall floored by mosses and vaulted with the branches of a stately beech. Through the terraces of low bushes, then the surrounding trees, the sough of the wind hardly reached it; the cry of birds was softened by distance and it was silent and withdrawn. Hrethric shivered. There was no ring of lords, no priest, no child Hrethric with his eyes screwed tight shut so that he should not see the climax of the ceremony. But it remained a sacred glade. It was mysterious, sheltering a deity who waited. Waited for Oslaf's pig. Hrethric looked down at the animal sleeping under his arm.

It was best to get it done quickly. He unlooped the sheaf from his neck and removed the thong. This he bound round the piglet's front legs, swung it to the ground and linked the thong over the rear hooves. Waking, it cried and rolled but soon growing tired, lay still, panting, its eyes staring in terror. Carrying the sheaf, Hrethric stepped over the moss and placed it against the thick bole of the beech. He laid his shield in the miniature pool held by the tree's arching roots. The slender lime wood floated, a blond disc at the base of the golden sheaf. They were the marks of the Scyldings, the men of the shield, descended from Sceaf, the sheaf. Then he returned to the piglet and dragged it towards the shrine.

The animal wriggled and squealed. He knelt and tried to keep it balanced on its spine, forcing the head back with one hand, but when he reached for his dagger, he lost his grip and the thing bucked and thrashed. Its bound hooves came up and scraped the hand pressed on its belly; its head swayed. Hampered by the dagger, he fought with both hands to pin it down and there was a screech of pain as the weapon's point scratched the pig's side. Then he had one hand muzzling its snout and the throat was pulsing with fear and muffled croaks. For a second he paused, halted by a vision of Oslaf's white neck squeezed by swart hands. Then the dagger ripped and blood gushed over the moss.

A twig cracked behind him. Bushes rustled and the blood in his veins set.

The night visitor had smelt him. He had seen his track through the leaves. He had heard the pig. He was pushing through the bushes now. He was approaching, his arms forward, ready to grab.

'No!' Hrethric shouted, swivelled round on his knee and jabbed.

Only the air received the cut of his knife.

'I will not harm you,' a man said.

15

# THREE

Hrethric scrambled to his feet, keeping his arm outstretched and scramasax pointing. This man was a stranger.

'I do not come before you as an enemy,' the man insisted. The expression was formal and sounded like an assurance often repeated and of which he had grown weary. He left the bushes and came closer. Seeing the small pool under the tree's roots, he knelt down and scooped up water in a cupped hand. He drank greedily but kept his back to Hrethric as if ashamed that the young man should witness his need.

'This is a shrine,' Hrethric reproached him.

'Yes; but however powerful your deity, I think there is little she could do to worsen my state,' he answered, self-mocking and tired. He rose and stood looking down at the quiet pig.

With his dagger still ready, Hrethric examined the stranger. The cloth binding his feet and calves was stiff with dried mud; his sandals, of a style sometimes brought by merchants, curled at the edge with too much wear, and their thongs bristled with knots where they had split; the fur hanging from his shoulders was matted and stained, and his tunic was spotted with grease. But the fur was secured by a large golden brooch; a jewelled buckle latched his belt; the fabric of his tunic was fine linen, and in spite of the crusting dirt, a gold thread occasionally shone through. And Hrethric knew what he was.

Apprehensive, he chose the polite term. 'You are a traveller?'

'I am an exile,' the stranger corrected him. 'Do not attempt to evade truth with inexact words. My exile is through misfortune, not dishonour. That I must ask you to believe. I have no proof.'

Hrethric was silent. The man's face was lined, unwashed and lean; the hand resting upon the trunk of the birch was placed there for support; but he returned Hrethric's regard without flinching and there was dignity in the set of his head; a man forced by circumstances to beg, but who would do so without whining, keeping his spirit whole. Slowly Hrethric wiped the pig's blood from his scramasax and returned it to its sheath. The man smiled, then again his eyes rested on the pig.

'You have not eaten today?'

'Today?' The stranger laughed harshly, then frowned, angered at what he had revealed.

'There is a village the other side of the track. You will find it if you follow the path. Wihtgar, the head churl, will give you gruel.' He had no knowledge of court etiquette concerning strangers. Now no one sought his father for shelter and protection. The young man smiled grimly at the ironic notion. Ruled by the terror of the night visitor, the kingdom was shunned.

'I have seen the village, but I did not ask for meat there. I could not take and leave another's belly cold.'

His integrity forced Hrethric's admission: 'This was Wihtgar's pig. It was necessary. I had to perform a sacrifice. I wish the deity to look kindly upon one who is dead.'

'I hope the deity looks kindly upon Wihtgar who gave up his pig. He needs her blessing more.'

He turned and began to walk back to his bundle left by the path. Provoked by his criticism, guilty, admitting that he had used his rank arrogantly, Hrethric called to him, 'I will reward him for it. I will send him another pig, better than this miserable thing. I am Hrethric, son of Hrothgar, son of Healfdene, of the Scylding people.'

The stranger stopped. 'They call me Angenga.'

'Angenga, one who goes alone?' the other murmured.

'Yes. Son of Aethelfrid, son of Aelle. And if you Hrethric, son of Hrothgar, inherit your father's generosity, I am sure you will give Wihtgar more than adequate compensation for his loss.'

'You have met my father?'

'No, but his reputation for giving reaches far beyond the boundaries of his kingdom. As does his fame in battle and his achievement as a powerful and just king.'

He described a Hrothgar whom the young man could barely recognize as his father. He knew him as a king powerless against the visitor's onslaughts, grey and sick with grief. He felt grateful to Angenga for quoting his father's past glories. Shyly, he answered, 'We have exchanged names. Now we should eat. Will you share this pig?'

'And the deity?' the man asked, keeping his face impassive.

'We will leave her the head. She will be satisfied. Besides, I too am hungry.'

Angenga smiled back. 'And people say that youth does not know how to compromise!' He looked round. 'A spit – that is what we need. A spit! A slender branch, green and full of sap, for a spit!' He began beating among the low bushes with his scramasax. 'The prospect of food makes me merry,' he stated unnecessarily.

18

This sudden change of mood surprised Hrethric; his gaiety was infectious, and when the young man went into the forest to search for kindling, he did not think of the hall visitor. Sometimes he prowled by day, would wait in lonely places unlit by the sun. Yet Hrethric whistled.

When he returned, loaded with dead wood, the fire was already burning. Angenga had turned back a rectangle of moss on the edge of the glade, as far away as possible from the shrine. 'It is a serene and lovely place. I do not wish to spoil its beauty. Neither do I wish to offend your deity, so we will eat far from her.' Again his companion was surprised. 'No, I am not inconsistent. I have little faith that the deity will be moved by the sacrifice of a pig, but I believe there is a force that rules the lives of men.'

He had cleaned the carcass and skewered it on a spit. It crackled and spat as the flames sprang under it. On the ground lay the stranger's scramasax, as splendid as any Hrethric had seen in the court of his father. Its silver hilt was etched with a pattern of interweaving cords and the pommel was covered with beaten gold decorated with the heads of birds whose beaks were inlaid with ivory and from whose eyes crimson garnets winked.

'A gift from my lord,' Angenga explained. 'No man could have had a better. Now he is dead and his thanes lie with him. I survived; but sometimes I think that life is the harder penalty.'

'Yes,' Hrethric agreed, but the moss was dappled with blobs of sunlight which twirled down through the swaying branches; his nostrils were full of the rich scent of the pig. 'All the same, roasted meat is good on a winter morning.'

'True, and all the better for being unexpected. I do not resist pleasure when it comes.' The heat was warming the weariness and pallor from the man's face; his hands were strong now and deft. Balancing fresh wood upon the radiant embers, keeping the funnel of flames under the spit, he hummed softly.

'Here's a riddle for you,' he announced. 'My tongue is silent but noise issues from my mouth. My breath has stopped but others take its fragrance. My skin feels nothing but it bubbles and runs with sweat. I have no wings but I spin in the air like a bird. What am I?'

'It doesn't look much like a bird,' the other laughed.

'I made it too easy. It is difficult to fashion things of the imagination when you are cooking. Your turn.'

'My belly is empty. I have weapons but do not hunt. I must wait as my mouth waters with longing. I dream that soon my prince will share his food.'

'That is just as easy, except that I am not dreaming,' and Angenga drew the carcass off the spit, cracked it down the spine with his scramasax, gave half to Hrethric, then, laying his portion on the grass between his feet, hacked off a chunk.

'But it isn't you!' cramming the first crisp strip into his mouth. 'It is Wihtgar!'

'Good! And so is this pig.'

They were not long eating.

'Tell me,' the man asked, carrying water from the pool and dousing the ashes, 'is it usual for the priest to allow another to do his office?'

'He is old and timorous. It is many winters since he ventured here.'

Angenga looked at him curiously. He rolled back the moss, then, 'So. Nothing is harmed. Your deity will not strike. I saw your face when I approached.'

'It was not the deity I thought I heard.' The night of waiting, the dank morning, Unferth, the bloodied water in the bucket, returned to him. The glade was no longer splashed with skipping light; the fire's flames were quenched; the man's humming had ceased. 'It was the night visitor.'

'Ah,' the man breathed. 'There are many. Sometimes, when the night is cold, one's sleep is tormented with spirits. There are the warriors who accuse, dragging themselves on hacked limbs to my bed; there are the companions whom the sword claimed; there is my lord who fell in the battle rushes; and other spirits who have no form or features. They are regrets and loneliness and sadness at the passing of fellowship and beauty. What is your night visitor?'

'He lives beyond the marshes. He comes out of the fastness searching for prey.'

'He cannot harm you. The fears of youth are many, but they will pass.'

'He comes with the mist, treading the lonely spaces where no one walks. In the night he comes to the great hall. No men sleep there now. After dusk it is deserted.'

'Even warriors fear this spirit?'

'He is no spirit. He is called Grendel.' The name scorched his tongue.

'Grendel.' The man's face was alert. 'Grendel. That is a name I have heard whispered. Is there no trap or sword that can overcome such a beast?'

'He is stronger and more hungry for blood than any beast. One night when I was three winters and the lords celebrated the birth of my brother Hrothmund, he burst into the hall and slaughtered thirty of the duguth, the tried warriors. That was the first time he came. Many since have stayed to fight with him. Troops of men would stand guard,

21

but they could not overcome him and most were killed. So it became the practice for the brave to confront the monster alone, because they wished to prevent the death of companions. Now it is the turn of the geogoth, the young and inexperienced in battle. We call it the night of waiting.' He looked towards the beech where the sheaf and shield lay in the roots' embrace.

'He was your friend?'

'Yes. Oslaf, son of Osric. He taught me to ride.'

'You must remember him for his friendship and courage, Hrethric.'

'Yes. He was braver than I. I have yet to say, "I will wait there. I will wait there for the king my father." And for Oslaf.' He was confiding in this stranger as he could have done to no one except his sister, Freawaru.

'There are many kinds of courage, and ways of showing it. Fighting is not the only one. This morning you came through the forest alone and performed what the priest would not dare.'

They had risen and were pushing through the bushes. 'Wait,' Hrethric restrained him. 'Do you hear?'

There were sounds, heavy and rhythmic. 'Only men marching,' he answered the alarm on the young man's face. 'Also a horse.'

They hurried down the path. By the time they were in sight of the wide track which ran from the beach to the court, the noise was almost upon them. They halted and stood concealed behind a fallen tree.

The horse came first, stepping down the centre of the track, paced by its rider to the measure of the men who walked behind. There were fourteen of them, grouped in twos and threes a little behind another who was clearly

22

their leader, and they were not merchants and their servants returning with goods to trade to their king, nor were they sailors, though their hair was lank with brine and their faces raw with spray and salt wind. They were fighters. They strode down the track looking neither to right nor left, upright and fearless. The sun glowed in the polished bosses of their shields, caught the flame-forged blades of their swords, and sparkled among the iron points of their spears. As they trod the passage between the bare trees they were a column of brightness, claiming the brief winter sun as their own and transforming its pale light into dazzling brilliance. The rings of their war corslets glimmered and clicked as they moved and the bronze of their helmets shimmered. Above the vizors, mounted on the crest of each helmet, a figure of a wild boar glinted. With feet firm and heads thrust forward, the boars arched ready, as powerful and resolute as the men who walked under their guard.

'A fine troop of men,' Angenga commented when they had passed. 'Wherever they have been, I am sure they have victory to report.'

'But they are not ours. I have never seen that company of duguth before.' Nor had he ever seen such warriors. His father's duguth no longer set out in their battle gear. 'Though I do not think they are hostile, do you?'

'No. The retainer on the horse was not one of them, was he? He rode easy, not like a man who was afraid or who purposed betrayal.'

'He is the guard on the farmost headland.'

'Then they come from the eastern sea:

> On far waters weaving,    the wave-fast vessel
> Bent to the breeze,    beaded with spray,

23

*Skimmed the green flood,   her prow foam-feathered,*
*Like white gull gliding,   grace on the wing.'*

'You are a scop?'

'Scop, bard, poet, versifier, word–weaver, spell–spinner, myth–maker, string–strummer – there are plenty of names.'

For the first time Hrethric noticed the shape of the thing he carried, laced inside the soft skin of a kid. To confirm his deduction, Angenga poked a finger through a gap and plucked at a string. 'A treasured possession,' he said.

'I should like to see it, but first let us follow the troop.'

They stepped out of the shadow of the trees on to the strip of sunlight along the track. It dipped ahead of them, concealing the warriors.

'I want to know why they have come here. Clearly the coast-guard thinks they have a good reason. He has allowed them to land and is leading them to the court.'

Hurrying forward with Hrethric, the scop improvised:

*'Then called to his comrades   the cliff-warden most trusted,*
*"Keep here the tide-sifter   safe under headland,*
*Guard well the carved prow   at painter restive,*
*Till neat clinker-keel   tight caulked for sea paths,*
*Bears in her bosom   the battle-proved strangers,*
*These warriors in war-gear   back to their home."*

A bit rough,' he added critically. 'That would need polishing.'

Hrethric laughed. 'It was reasonably convincing though, Angenga, particularly when we take into account that you have not seen their ship, nor did you witness how the men were received.'

His companion smiled back. 'The piece is the usual

24

mixture of fancy, observation and good sense, and you have admitted that it is plausible. After all, their boat cannot be very different from other boats, and no host would leave it on a foreign shore without some guarantee, certainly not a host led by that man we have just seen.'

'And what of him? What words can you find for him?'

'Ah, that is another matter. I would not venture even a line on such a slight acquaintance.'

They were walking fast; ahead of them the company was nearing the edge of the forest. 'You surprise me, Angenga. You must have received an impression. Why do you hesitate over him when you can fashion lines about an incident you have not seen?'

'Men must be studied and understood. When I tell my stories I may alter things, or places, or what has happened, but I never tamper with men. I set them out as they are. Their nature is the fabric of my craft and if I meddled with that I should lose their trust.' Then he added more lightly, 'All the same, it is perhaps a good thing that they do not always recognize themselves.'

'Your silence disappoints me.'

'You do not need my opinion about him, Hrethric. You have already formed your own and want me to confirm it; and your eagerness teaches me something else.'

'What is that?'

'That the man can fascinate and draw others to him.'

They had reached the end of the forest. The duguth were striding away in the distance and the coast guard was riding back. He stopped and inclined his head in deference to his prince.

'Who are these warriors, Cerdic?'

'They are men of the Geats, my lord.'

'Why do they come? You should not leave them to march with their equipment across our land.'

'I must return to the coast, my prince. It is a long journey and I cannot ride after dusk,' he defended. 'They do not come for battle. They are warriors from the court of Hygelac and have a mission to our king. They are honourable. The king your father has never had cause to question my judgement. Their leader does not come as an enemy or a spy or a wandering exile.' He dug his heels into his horse's flanks and cantered off.

Hrethric's face flushed at the discourtesy to his companion. The guard was one of Unferth's men.

'He does his work well,' Angenga reasoned to him. 'It is his duty to be alert and the king is well served by such a man. I must go now. I hope that the deity smiles upon you and that some day the evil thing that visits your nights will be removed. Meanwhile your place is in your father's court, Hrethric.'

He stood aside, waiting for the young man to pass, and Hrethric knew that he had initiated this parting to save the prince further embarrassment. He was taken with pity for the man's loneliness, for his harsh, comfortless life. 'I should like you to be my guest in the court. If you accept, you must repay me with a song for the geogoth who waited.'

It seemed a long time before the scop answered. 'Thank you for the condition, Hrethric. I will come.'

As they emerged from the trees the court was before them. It was the court of day without mist or shadows. Churls and retainers bustled between the buildings; women ground corn and cooked beside the huts; an occasional thane rode across the space in the centre. But gradually this activity ceased. One by one the people scattered over the knoll heard the sound of the troop approaching. They stopped their work, rose or straightened; tools or cooking utensils hung forgotten from the still hands; two thanes reined in their horses; all stared towards the company of warriors striding down the track at the base of the small hill. Everyone was silent; no one called out a warning or command. All were motionless; none reached for a weapon or rushed to prevent the passage of the strangers.

Yet the clearing pulsed with sound and throbbed with movement, with the thud of the men's feet on the earth and the muscular swing of their limbs, with the clash of their swords and the sway of their shields, with the clink of their ringed corslets and the dip and jab of their spears. While light darted from their helmets, glittered on every part of their armour and advanced with them, striking the winter air and framing the group of strangers in a compact, luminous haze.

They reached the avenue of trees which led to the hall, wheeled, and started to ascend it, taking the slope easily without slackening their pace. Hrethric watched them, saw the fighters march up the avenue which was Grendel's way, and which for the space of eight winters he had not dared to tread. He turned to the scop but his eyes were not following the troop. They had slid ahead and were regarding the hall which was the men's goal.

'Ah,' he breathed.

From their position at the base of the knoll, they looked upward and across towards the massive wooden doors. The hinges and latches were clearly visible, heavy but lustrous in the winter light. Hewn from the core of the straightest oaks, the thick panels of the walls fitted tightly together without use of daub and gleamed with the polish of the craftsman's chisel. The roof, a high wedge of thick thatch, was smooth and shone as worked gold, and at its peak above the doors the gables crossed and stretched upwards, carved like antlers and inlaid with tusks and the finest horn.

'My father built it,' Hrethric told him, suddenly proud. 'It is there that the monster comes. None feasts or sings in it after dusk.'

'Perhaps he envies you for possessing it. The laughter and feasting of men are hateful to him. He is lonely in his wickedness.'

They stood together in silence, looking beyond the arc of court chambers towards the great hall. Huge and strong it commanded, firmly rooted at the head of the slope, but its golden roof reached into the sky, crowned by the grace of the branched gables.

'How is it named?' the scop asked.

'We call it Heorot.'

'Heorot,' the man repeated. 'Heorot, the Stag.'

# FOUR

There was a stir beside one of the apartments and a horseman rode out. From the sheen of his mantle worn for ceremonies, Hrethric recognized Wulfgar, the herald, cantering across the open space to meet the strangers at the doors of the hall.

'You must come to my mother, Angenga,' Hrethric said.

Standing in her chamber, she was already preparing for the summons to council. A woman was burnishing the wide gold collar; another was pinning on the right shoulder of her gown a brooch which matched another over her left breast; Freawaru held the strings of translucent beads which would hang in heavy loops between the two brooches. Usually dull and silent after the night of waiting, the chamber glinted with winking gold and gems and hummed with busyness and chatter.

'You have brought one of the strangers?' Wealhtheow asked.

'He is a stranger, Mother, but not one of the host. He is Angenga, son of Aethelfrid, son of Aelle. He journeys alone.'

Conscious of her disappointment, the scop looked beyond her as she examined him, giving her time to recognize the significance of the stained clothing together with the gold clasps and the leather scabbard bound with bronze; but there was nothing servile in his posture and he did not blush under her regard.

'It is many winters since one such as you has come to

29

our kingdom. There was a time when men sought my lord, knowing that he would give them shelter and, if their cause was good, a place in the hall. Now all he has to offer is sorrow and death.'

'Your son has told me of Grendel,' the scop answered quietly and saw that, even within her apartment in the day's light, Wealhtheow flinched. A moan came from one of the women.

'Yes. So what man would hope for land or a home among the Scyldings?'

'I look for neither. My land is where my lord fell in battle. My home is the memory of his love and comradeship. I have done nothing that is dishonourable, no crime, or murder, or treachery, nothing to cause me shame. All I ask, lady, is that I may be allowed to pass freely through your kingdom.'

'That you may do, and you may stay in the court for as long as you wish, though our affliction makes us joyless hosts. Now I will give you a gift.'

She tumbled the contents of a casket upon the soft cloth which covered the trestle and scooping up amulets, hoops of gold, brooches and slender collars, let them run through her fingers in a living, coloured stream. 'What will you have? Unlike this gold, the custom of giving has rusted through lack of use. It is a long time since I made a gift to a stranger.'

'And it is long since I received a gift from a queen. But I would prefer to accept none of these. May I beg the chatelaine at your belt? Its value is greater than a precious gem, for what it bears has served the beauty of a queen and gentle woman.'

'It is not often that anyone flatters to obtain less than is offered,' she replied, but her cheeks had flushed at the scop's compliment and her hand lingered as she placed the chatelaine upon his open palm. Leaning against one of the wooden pillars, Hrethric suddenly saw her not only as a queen and mother, but as a woman who charmed his sex and quickly gained its affection. He thought of Hrothulf and something in his mind shied like a horse at a movement beside a dark path.

Angenga thanked her and stroked the fine wires from which hung a pair of tweezers, a sharp horn blade, small iron scissors, a sliver of polished amber for nails and cuticles, several slender bone needles, an ivory comb with the figure of a hart incised down the centre, the antlers spreading and curling through the curves of its leaping legs. 'Is it so surprising that I asked for this? Looking as I do, I shall find it more useful than any jewel.'

She laughed. She supported herself against the trestle and the sound of her unexpected gaiety whirled round the chamber, repeated by her children and women. Then Wulfgar was at the door, bringing the message from the king that the council was about to begin. Traditionally formal, the herald answered her questions concerning the host: 'They are warriors from the kingdom of the Geats, my queen. They come not in enmity but friendship and their leader has requested an audience with our king,' but as he mounted his horse, the solemnity of his office slipped away and he hurried, his expression eager and vivacious.

'What can this mean?' she demanded. 'What friendship can they offer or we give in return? For a moment my spirit was lightened; I dressed myself for the council, but now these jewels seem vain, the meaningless trappings of a sovereign without power. We cannot disguise our weakness. We cannot hide from these men that our kingdom is subject to an evil that is without cure. There is no family that does not mourn a death or worse misery. Hrothmund, my son who was born on the first night of the visitor, he is a cursed thing, sickly and strange. Nothing can save us. Men die. We offer sacrifices, but the deity does not listen. How can I meet these men without shame?' She was appealing to the scop.

'You can, my lady. There is no shame where there is no guilt. I am an exile, but I can meet your eyes and assure you that is true. I have seen these warriors. They are fresh and assured. Their leader is a man to be reckoned with. Yet he waits. He waits to be received by a queen.'

Encouraged, she smiled at him. 'Thank you, Angenga,' and drawing a ring from a finger, 'This is my gift, and I do not give it to a stranger, but to a friend.' Taking his hand, she pushed the slim circlet over a chapped knuckle. As she did so, a shadow cut between them.

'I have come to escort you to the hall,' Hrothulf announced.

Startled, she swung round like one accused, while he showed his contempt for her companion by the sneering pinch of his lips.

'Hrothgar is ready.' He emphasized the name. 'The matter is urgent. This is no time for idle talk.'

His comment angered her, but she did not answer. Accepting a fur cloak from Freawaru, she drew it close over her breasts.

'My daughter will take you to a chamber,' she said to Angenga. 'And Hrethric, you must accompany us to the council. It is time you learnt its customs.'

So Hrethric followed behind them, conscious of the new honour, not caring that his cousin disapproved. He was impatient to hear the leader of these unbidden warriors for whom the day itself had changed, had transformed itself out of the dank steam of dawn into a noon which was dry and brisk. They had brought with them the sharp, ringing clarity of a winter sky in which the sun, like a flaming shield, licked the thatch of Heorot into molten gold. Down in the work hut of the smith, they had added a tune to the beat of his hammer, and upon the faces of churls and retainers they had bestowed a shy hope.

In the centre of Heorot a low fire was burning. Its meagre light fell against the pillars which flanked the hearth and stretched, chiselled and carved, down the length of the hall like a continuation of the living trees that lined the avenue outside. Shadows from these hewn trunks striped the side aisles and angled up the walls where the noon light from the doors was diluted, colourless and thin. Counsellors stood by the benches between the pillars; they sat when Wealhtheow and Hrothulf took their places on the high seat, one on each side of the king. Sitting nearer the door, at the opposite end to his father's throne, Hrethric calculated that the assembly was bigger than usual. Thanes and the remaining duguth had been invited, in addition to the counsellors who sat with Hrothgar or formed a group below him.

'You know why I have called this council,' Hrothgar began. 'You have seen the company of warriors. Wulfgar reports that they are men of the Geats and they have come together in one ship and bring no other troops. One of them is not entirely a stranger, their leader, whose name is Beowulf. That name will mean nothing to the younger ones among you, though he spent some winters here as a child. You remember Ecgtheow?' he addressed the older men beside him, and was answered by nods. A few eyebrows were raised. 'That was a time when this court had influence amongst the tribes.'

He paused and reached for the goblet by his hand. Addressing the whole assembly again, he continued, 'Ecgtheow became involved in a feud with the Wylfings and Hrethel could not harbour him; his presence in the Geat court was too dangerous. So he sought refuge here with his lady and the child Beowulf. Eventually I settled the feud. I sent gifts to the Wylfings and compensation for their dead, and Ecgtheow was allowed to return to his country. Since then our relations with the Geats have been cordial and we have exchanged gifts, though nothing has passed between us for these many winters.

'Now we are visited by a deputation from their present king, Hygelac. Aeschere has taken the troop to quarters and has attended to their needs but before I invite in their leaders, there may be some of you who wish to speak.'

'Yes.' Unferth's response was immediate. During Hrothgar's speech he had been restless, his eyes going to and fro across the faces which had turned without exception upon their king. 'What if this man, this Beowulf, conceals a private reason for coming? He is his father's son. Some of his kinsmen were killed by the Wylfings. He may hope to continue the feud from our shores. From what I see of him and the equipment he carries, he has not the appearance of a man of peace.' He looked round and a number of the duguth sniggered.

'His case will be judged on its merits,' Hrothgar answered wearily. 'In this life the veins of many men stream with the blood of a feud.'

Hrethric saw his mother stiffen and for a moment their

eyes touched. Would Freawaru's promised marriage to Ingeld succeed in its purpose? Would his tribe accept her as a mark of friendship, all past wars forgotten, or was Freawaru doomed?

'We cannot risk sheltering a troop of fighters who may provoke others to attack us,' Unferth was continuing. 'We possess a mere handful of duguth; we have scarcely enough men to guard the coast. Our affliction makes us vulnerable to hostile bands.'

'It also protects us,' the king pointed out. 'None dares to invade a kingdom where he may meet a thing more terrible and deadly than any host. It ensures our isolation. We are as removed from men's hate as we are from their love.' Again his hand took the goblet which, drained, a retainer immediately refilled.

'But not if we harbour men whom others seek, men on whom others must wreak their vengeance.' His reasoning was diplomatic and sensible but there was a falsity in his tone. Unferth was always informed ahead of everyone else. The coastguard was under his influence and would have sent a message. Hrethric suspected that it was not the safety of the kingdom that worried the counsellor, but the presence of the troop's leader.

'I believe that this warrior's purpose is not selfish. Perhaps he hopes to repay his debt to me who once gave his family a place in this hall. We will decide what action we take when we have heard him,' and the king gestured to Wulfgar to admit the Geat.

Silenced, Unferth tapped his scramasax and glared at the assembly but his supporters, like the rest of the council, were looking towards the doors, craning to see the entrance of their guest. Anticipation passed along them like the

35

spring's breath warming the trees into bud. And it was not disappointed.

He strode down the hall like a man elect. His carriage was proud. His face, stern. His eyes skimmed over the thanes who lined his passage and gave them neither acknowledgement nor heed. Tough, powerful, he paced the wooden floor of Heorot. The muscles in his calves were moulded hard; his neck was ridged with sinews; the corslet took the swell of his massive shoulders. Reaching the high seat, he stood with feet gripping the floor as if he possessed it, a man who bore his body like a thing loved by the gods.

'Good health to you, Hrothgar, King of the Scyldings.' The voice came deep out of the chest's drum. 'I am Beowulf, son of Ecgtheow and nephew of Hygelac, King of the Geats.'

'Your person is worthy of your father and the gentle lady who bore you. You were a child when you last ate with us in our hall.'

'That I scarcely remember but my parents taught me of your kindness.' He paused, then, preliminaries over, he gave his description. 'I am a fighter. My skill is famous over many lands. There is no one who can match it. I have fought for Hygelac and defeated many of his enemies. My success was due both to my strength and to my leadership, for men are inspired to follow me against hosts which before quelled their brave swords. I come now with a troop of men to rid you of the monstrous thing which has occupied your kingdom these twelve winters.' Startled, men jerked back as if from a blow then leant forward again, their faces intense and expectant.

'Already I have accomplished great feats of daring. Now

I challenge your loathsome enemy. I and my men will fight your demon, Grendel.'

The name dashed against the rafters, scattered the logs along the hearth into a flurry of sparks, and creaked through the benches where men glanced over shoulders to the doors. The high posts still framed the daylight and Beowulf, straight and unmoving, kept his eyes on the king.

'Your courage is great,' Hrothgar answered him. The skin on his face was slack over the sharp bones; for each thane that Grendel had consumed, there had passed from him a drop of his blood, a curve of his flesh. But now a faint colour lay in the hollows of his cheeks. 'However, you must understand that this is no ordinary foe, though he is shaped in the likeness of a man. His size surpasses that of any creature with which heroes have contended in former ages. His strength and power are not drawn from the good things of Nerthus, our earth mother, from the spring which garlands the land with flowers, from the sun which fattens the gold grain on its stalk, from the moon which silvers the waters. No, he feeds upon her poisonous vapours, upon the stifling mists which rise from her lower regions, upon the slime of her marshes, upon the sweat of her darkness, and his body is ribbed with the steel of her frost.'

'That is how the demon is reported. It troubles me little. My reputation does not rest solely on my victories over men. I have fought with beings that men called giants. I have killed beasts of the sea so huge that they could split the keel of a ship as they reared out of the depths. It is for this reason that my kin and uncle did not hinder me when he knew my wish.' His voice was impatient, a little querulous, and his eyes, sweeping along the faces of the counsellors, reached Hrothulf.

'Perhaps you think I boast,' he addressed him. 'What I say is the truth and will not be denied by any man I bring.'

'I do not doubt your words,' the other answered with a smile meant to flatter, 'but I am puzzled. I am surprised that a man like yourself, who enjoys such notoriety – fame – and who shows such virtuosity in adventure, I am surprised that he brings with him a company of duguth.'

'That is customary,' Wealhtheow interrupted sharply.

'Indeed, retainers are necessary, but surely he does not need the help of a company to fight our evil? If he is endowed with such strength, why does not Beowulf challenge the monster to single combat?'

At one end of the high seat a mouth laughed with approval though no sound issued from it, then Unferth was again masked by the hearth's smoke.

'Who is it that asks this question?' Beowulf demanded.

'I am Hrothulf, son of Halga, who was brother of our king,' he replied, resuming the formal speech of the council.

'So, you too are nephew of your lord. I hope your king can trust in the service of his kinsman, as mine can, in times of need. And, Hrothulf, nephew of the King of the Scyldings, I Beowulf, nephew of Hygelac, will tell you how, here in this court, I shall bring honour and acclaim to my Geat lord.

'I shall fight your demon alone. My duguth will defend only themselves, if that is necessary. More: I shall wear neither ringed armour nor helmet. Sword and shield shall be laid aside. I shall grapple with him, strength for strength, grip for grip, muscle against muscle.'

Consternation and approval swelled through the hall. Hrothgar said, 'We do not ask this of you, Beowulf. Such courage is admirable but should be guided by wisdom.'

'It is my wish. I challenge your monster.' He stared at Hrothulf who, pleased with his success in provoking the Geat, responded with a brief, amused nod. 'I ask your permission to fight him and that only my duguth remain with me in this hall this night.'

The king sighed and his hand sought the full cup. 'Very well. It shall be arranged as you wish. If you succeed, you will be well rewarded. Is there anything more you wish to ask of me?'

'No; I have no other request. I am told that this Grendel devours his victims upon these benches or carries them off to feast upon in his lair.' One of Hrothgar's hands covered his face while the other reached again for the cup. 'If my strength fails, then I say that I deserve such an end.'

As he spoke, he turned and regarded the men sitting on the benches which that morning had been spattered with the blood of Oslaf and which had dripped with the blood of countless others who had waited; but he did not see the sad ghosts crowding the spaces, only admiration and wonder; and he did not hear the scream of death and the sorrowful wailing, but the shouts of men's praise.

He inclined his head in acknowledgement, then again faced the high seat.

With both hands round the goblet, Hrothgar said quietly, 'The council's thanks are repeated by their king, but you must excuse me when I cannot shout as they do. For twelve winters greedy death has haunted my nights and grief has entered my chamber on each bloodstained dawn. This hall, which I built to delight the eyes of my people and as a fit home for feasting and song, my Heorot, is now stripped of its ornaments and is a place of terror and slaughter. Its beauty is disfigured and accuses me like a woman ravished

39

by a brute. Kill our night visitor, Beowulf, and you will not only save the living but you will restore the glory of this hall.'

As he concluded, Hrothgar stretched out both his hands towards the young warrior, and the goblet, forgotten, crashed down. Wine ran between the king's fingers, spread across the surface of the table and trickled red gouts at the Geat's feet. Clumsily, with hands shaking, Hrothgar righted the cup and his son saw Hrothulf's expression of contempt and the newcomer's chin tilted high with disdain.

Pushing through the thanes around him, Hrethric reached the doors. He stood looking down the wide avenue, his teeth clenched. While behind him Aeschere called to retainers to bring food; Wealhtheow rose to welcome Beowulf, and his father sat bowed and silent before the Geat who had witnessed his frailty. A Scylding mocked by his nephew and who needed the support and courage of a powerful son.

# FIVE

'This is good news,' the scop commented by his side.

'Yes; but it should be me. It should be me who stands before my father. It should be me offering my strength.'

'You must be patient, Hrethric. Fifteen years are not long enough to form a man capable of opposing your night creature.'

'Oslaf did. Oslaf was permitted. He was barely two winters older than I.'

'So this morning you killed a pig,' Angenga answered sharply. 'You are speaking like a child. Petulance is no substitute for strength. I have heard of this man. His reputation has spread even so far as the lands bordering the northern sea. His fights, his daring, are material for gossip and stories amongst travellers and seamen. Look at him.' He swung Hrethric round to face the interior of the hall where Beowulf stood by the hearth, feet astride, watching retainers drag tables between the high pillars. 'Look at those shoulders. Look at that neck. Look at that jaw. He could crush the spine of a wolf between his teeth. And that man has yet to be proved. He has not yet killed Grendel.'

'It should be one of us, a Scylding. It should not be a Geat who removes our disgrace.'

'Many have tried. Perhaps it is a task for a stranger.'

'Will he succeed?'

'I am a scop, not a prophet, Hrethric. Certainly he has much in his favour. We must await the outcome.'

Escorted by Wulfgar, the company of Geats had just joined their leader and together they followed Aeschere to the seats above the hearth traditionally reserved for guests, and for many years empty. Wiped clean of the film of salt from their journey, their corslets shone even more brightly in the firelight; their iron swords lay easy but ready against their thighs and each man carried his helmet like a possession cherished for its use and splendour. These Geats were trim, professional, built for their craft.

'You are right. I would have no chance against the demon,' Hrethric admitted. 'All the same, I wish I could undertake this danger, for my father's sake.'

'There are others which you may have to face one day. I know a little. I have spoken with Freawaru.'

They had taken their seats. By their sides, the benches were filling with thanes; lower down were grouped the geogoth, the young men of the court. Those who had not attended the council were stretching to see the Geats; everyone was alert; Beowulf's challenge had made them almost gay. But they were not relaxed, ready for an evening of wine and stories, for the day was passing and habit kept them nervous, glancing towards the doors, checking each slight gradation in the diminishing light. Retainers hurried with dishes and goblets, less in order to serve quickly than to ensure that their duty was soon completed, and the food had been prepared hastily, dried meat swiftly roasted, the barley in the cakes coarsely ground. This was no feast but a meal to be taken in haste, a race before the terror of the manacling night.

Their guests noted this, but for Hrethric it was commonplace, a routine he was bred to and so did not notice, as inevitable as court etiquette and the ceremony of public speech. This hurry was no more extraordinary than what he saw at the end of the table in front of the high seat, but today his habitual fear at the sight was sharpened, this day of the Geats' arrival, this day of Beowulf's oath. Biting into the meat pierced by his dagger, Hrethric watched.

Turned away from their companions, two figures leaned together. The folds of their mantles were flattened and made dull by the twilight; their faces were indistinct; but as they bent forward to observe first the king and then the Geats feasting below him, the foreheads of the two men were glazed like grease by a flame which thrust suddenly from a log in the hearth, and their slanting features were black shadows bordered by the skulls' bones. They talked a little longer, then Hrothulf rose and returned to his seat by the king while Unferth stepped from the dais and took up a position at the fire.

'Let us drink to Beowulf and his company of duguth,' he called out. The noise in the hall faded. The Scyldings stood up, holding their goblets.

'I, Unferth, counsellor of the king, lead the Scyldings in a toast to Beowulf the Geat. May the deity grant him success this night and when the day breaks may he come safely out of this hall.'

Goblets were raised, wine tossed back, and Beowulf's name repeated again and again down the tables, but Hrethric caught a glimpse of a hand beckoning. Behind the high seat, Hrothulf was whispering to a retainer and gesturing to others. They nodded and, collecting more flagons of wine, approached the Geats and filled up their cups.

Though Unferth waved the assembly to sit down, his manner did not invite them to resume their feasting.

Outlined by the rippling flames, his figure was impenetrable and secret. His shadow jabbed across the floor.

'If you, son of Ecgtheow, rid us of the hall visitor, you will be honoured as the greatest of warriors. Today you have undertaken to fight the enemy without armour or sword, an impressive boast but better made by one who has never been defeated by either beasts or men. In fact, it interests me, purely, understand, from the point of view of your progress as a fighter. Has your skill increased more than was anticipated in your youth, or are there fewer men with the talent and power of Breca?'

'It pleases me that Breca's reputation has reached your kingdom. He was indeed a powerful swimmer.'

'So powerful, was he not, that he defeated you in that famous contest?'

'In a matter between friends there is neither defeat nor victory. Perhaps he who brought the story to you was ignorant of that fact.'

'And Beowulf is wise to dismiss the story. Who would wish to recount the follies and failures of one's youth?' Unferth addressed the Scyldings. His look jerked up and down the benches, prodding his supporters to acquiesce as he belittled the new man.

'I will recount them, with Beowulf's permission.' Angenga had risen, his mantle thrown back from his shoulders. 'I have heard the story of the occasion that Beowulf and Breca swam together. It is very suitable for a feast which honours your present guest.' He was looking round him, his hands gesturing. The hurry and tension of the assembly slackened and his audience smiled as they anticipated pleasure. Grendel was forgotten. 'It concerns two young men, headstrong but strong in muscle too, who

44

dared each other to swim the straits by their land and who for seven nights fought against the swell of waves and the toss of the storm-driven sea. Each carried a sword to protect him against the ocean creatures and one, your guest, killed many in threshing combat upon the sea's floor. The story has many beauties. You would watch the winter waves buffet the straining bodies; you would see the beasts writhing—'

'Who is this stranger?' Unferth interrupted, whipping the attention back to himself. Now that he was washed, dressed in fresh clothes, Angenga's state was no longer obvious.

'He is Angenga, son of Aethelfrid.' It was difficult for Hrethric to oppose Unferth but he rose and stood beside the scop. Their shoulders touched. 'He is my guest. He carries a lyre on his journeys but today he came to this hall carrying something more precious, a gift from my mother, the queen.'

Hrothgar glanced at Wealhtheow, then nodded. Before taking his seat again, Hrethric saw his cousin leave his place by the king and quietly descend the dais.

'We welcome a friend of the prince.' Unferth modulated his tone to a forced courtesy. 'It is good to know there is a bard who can provide entertainment at a feast. After a day's work there is nothing like an absorbing tale to coax us into forgetting our cares and the harsh reality outside, but do not let us confuse fairy stories with fact. I suspect that this bard would have us believe things which are untrue.'

'Facts, your facts, are as pliable as churls,' Angenga replied slowly. 'I do not deal in lies. My duty is to discover what rests in the heart; my purpose is to reveal what I have found, by any means that I can employ.'

Smoke gushed suddenly from the base of the logs,

momentarily wreathing Unferth with strings of ochre through which his face stared yellow and pinched. 'We are growing too serious for this company. I do not question your skill as a manipulator of words but simply caution your hearers to remember that they are listening to fiction.'

'No one needs to be cautioned against my fairy stories, as you call them. It is true that they may lull men into forgetting but when they again confront hardships and despair they will remember something that rose from my stories and tugged at their minds: the spirit and endurance of man.'

Breaths were drawn in to applaud but hissed out wordlessly at a look from Unferth. 'I believe you, for men are easily deceived by sentiment and you would arrange your story to fit your purpose. But I am no poet. I am a plain counsellor in the Scylding court, and it seems to me that your method alters what really occurred. For example, you describe the match between Beowulf and Breca as a youthful escapade to which they dared each other. It was not. It was a competition arising from childish boasts. You describe them as headstrong, an endearing word. They were indeed, but they were also something more important: foolish. You referred to fights against whales and sea monsters, flattering our guest and wooing us to forget the swimming match. It was no part of your business to tell us that it was Breca who was the stronger swimmer, Breca who first reached the shore, Breca who won the contest. It is Breca whom we should praise.'

There were gasps along the benches and all heads swivelled, questioning, to Beowulf's place. But he was already on his feet, towering above them. 'The scop speaks well. It is you who twists the truth,' and though his voice was steady, the muscles in his throat pulsed.

'Breca was my friend. What we undertook when we swam together was no contest. We were not rivals; neither of us sought to prove that he was better in combat against the flood. We were young men then, our limbs, our sinews, our very entrails strained to use their manhood and we pledged ourselves to take the ocean's currents with our arms, to pit our bodies against the rage of the open sea. And this we did, in fellowship and joy. Together we met the waves which pitched, force against force. They crashed down and shattered upon our backs. Together we faced the rush of the turbulent winds. They parted at our shoulders' thrust. So for the space of five nights. Then the sea was torn by tempest. It gathered up the waves into solid cliffs which arched above us, then flung down, rolling us in coils of icy foam. The waters folded under us, opened in fissures which sucked us deep into the belly of the sea. It was then that Breca and I were separated. The swell parted us, and each one wondered whether the greedy flood was swollen with a new corpse.'

He paused. No one interrupted. Unferth was a dark figure shrunk into his mantle. Angenga was seated again, his lips quivering with satisfaction he could not wholly suppress. The eyes of everyone were fixed on Beowulf and, as he continued, the quick breathing of men was the only hint of movement except for a hand which lifted a flagon and tipped more wine into the goblets of the Geat warriors. Hrothulf, sitting now at their table, raised his cup. 'To your leader,' Hrethric heard him say, soft and pleasant, and Beowulf's company were obliged to drink.

'But the hungry ocean was not allowed to claim us. Fate had not decreed that our young bodies should soften and rot on the ocean's bed, for she looks favourably upon those who confront danger without fear. Yet she reserved a test for me greater than any my youth had suffered. While the ridged sea threw up Breca upon the shore, it dragged me into the clutch of sea monsters tossed from their sandy lairs by the swirl of the storm. Frenzied with rage, they took me for their foe and bore down upon me. The tempest lifted the sea. I was hurled against waves which emptied their waters over me and as they closed above my head one creature seized me between its teeth and pulled me down, down through the ferns and forests and rocky ranges of the sea. Until, panting with its burden, it reached the sandy floor and there lay for a moment resting before beginning the feast.

'It was then that I freed myself from its grip, prising open its jagged mouth with these hands, and at last I stood unhampered by waves ready to oppose its leaping thrust. For, its gorge throbbing for more taste of my blood, it came at me, teeth menacing, tail slicing, the draught of its heavy body scooping the sand into a fog of whirling grit through which I jabbed and saw the blood burst out and fly like a streamer among the branches of the ocean's trees. Maddened by pain, the beast jerked aside then swung back, ploughed great furrows in the sea bed as it made for me, and reared its head. It fell like a ship's prow upon me and I lay stunned under its weight.

'At last, as the current lifted it up, I rose and saw its throat impaled upon my sword and the blood gushing upward from the mortal wound. So I killed the first of the sea monsters. But the rest, swimming down on the red track of its anguish, attacked me in the same manner and through the mire of the sand-laden water and the dusk of the sea's floor darkened to night by the pall of their blood, I conquered each one, and dead and dying they floated with me to the surface and were later cast upon the shore.'

This time nothing could arrest the applause. The hall resounded with shouts, with the clank of goblet against goblet, with the drumming of fists upon tables; and Hrothulf, lounging comfortably with the Geats, nodding and smiling like an old friend, raised his cup for a toast, first placing a full one in the hand of the warrior who lolled against him. While Beowulf, not looking at his troop, bowed his head in response but remained standing.

As the noise decreased, he added, 'So, you understand, my friends, that though Breca swam well and was the first to reach land, he was not better than I. He did not fight sea beasts in the pummelling storm and the blinding depths of the sea. You, Unferth, were wrong to introduce this story and compel me to compare my power and courage with that of my friend, for I have heard stories about you which no malice can falsify. I know, Unferth, that you slew a kinsman, that you have the mark of murder on your brow, and yet you are allowed to walk freely in this court.'

Shocked, his listeners rustled and the scop rose as if to stay further accusation, but Beowulf ignored them all and the anger that had been contained now burst out and beat upon their heads.

'You, the slayer of a kinsman, you who goes unpunished, you who sits daily in council and have no remedy to offer your king, you, Unferth, think to mock the courage of Beowulf, son of Ecgtheow. You suggest that I am not capable of confronting Grendel, you whose spirit is so feeble that you cannot lift your sword against the enemy of your king. The Scyldings are not well served by such a counsellor.

Through your example they cower at the very name of Grendel and fly for refuge from his malignity. Not so we Geats. Our spirit is like our swords, forged in heat and hammered to keen iron, and I Beowulf, nephew of Hygelac, King of the Geats, will overcome this demon whom no Scylding has had the power or the ability to subdue.'

As he finished, a great din thundered down the tables. Goblets were knocked over; dishes were thrust aside; benches were overturned; men grabbed their daggers, leapt upon trestles and jostled to reach the hearth were the Geat company, stupefied by wine, blinked without comprehension and Beowulf, barred by the swords of Hrothulf and Unferth, stood steady and calculating, all muscles flexed.

Then a voice slashed through the tumult. 'Return to your places,' Hrothgar commanded. 'You shame the honour of the Scyldings. It is for me to make answer to our guests.'

In the silence he descended the dais and walked through his warriors and though he leant upon Aeschere's arm and his hand trembled, he was for a moment the Hrothgar of former times whose people followed at a word and whose enemies cringed under his sword. 'My friend, your speech is harsh to my ears. Once I, too, would have drawn and claimed the first thrust. But adversity has rusted my sword in its scabbard and makes me a beggar. I look upon this beloved hall, my Heorot, and see it stripped of its adornments. It is a shell which we inhabit by day and which at night is a den fouled by the hatred of the monstrous man-beast. Many have tried to rescue its beauty but, as you say, they have failed. Now you, who are not of our people, have come to oppose the demon and we are grateful. Never before have I left this hall in the care of a man who is not a Scylding. May fate be kind to you in this venture and your arm serve your strong spirit. But now day shrinks under the branches of the winter trees and the marsh lands ooze beneath the night stalker's tread. We go to our apartments, wishing you success tonight in Heorot.'

His reminder changed the postures of the Scyldings. Fear replaced aggression and they scrambled down from the tables, pushed scramasaxes hastily into their sheaths, elbowed one another and cursed the slowness of those in front delayed by their king's unhurried steps. As the place emptied, retainers quickly pulled tables and benches to the walls, gathered up goblets and dishes and laid out bolsters for the Geats. Then they scurried away, leaving Beowulf and his small troop alone in the vast hall.

But the scop lingered by the door and Hrethric, made bolder by his example, stayed with him. 'May fate bless your strength this night,' Angenga said down the long aisle.

'I think that is decreed. You spoke well for me at the supper, Scop, and I thank you.'

'Deeds are past for me. Speech is all I have left, but I know also the value of silence and I would not have scorned my hosts in their own court.'

Beowulf shrugged. 'It was true, what I said. I have come to perform a service for the king, not flatter his people. They are cowards and that counsellor is nothing – a paltry schemer envious of my vigour.'

'He is more than that. Do not underrate him, or the nephew his companion. Without your notice they have ensured that you will have no help tonight.'

They regarded his troop whose heads dropped then jerked back as they tried to attend; their bodies lurched; their mouths were slack. One more sodden with wine than the rest slithered off the bench as he stretched for a bolster and scrambled at Beowulf's feet. Violently his leader pulled him up.

'Remove my corslet, Hondscio,' he commanded harshly, willing the man to control, but while Hondscio stood with shoulders steadied by the other's fierce grip, his hands could not lift the heavy mail. Beside the hearth, surrounded by his sprawling men, Beowulf was a lonely figure. Their drunkenness was a desertion worse than flight and Hrethric was ashamed that a Scylding had brought this upon a guest. At least Oslaf, though younger, slighter, lacking the Geat's assurance and experience, had not fought the demon to the rhythm of wine-drenched snores or stumbled over the indifferent bodies of men he called his friends.

'I will stay with you, Beowulf of the Geats,' he heard himself say. 'I am Hrethric, son of Hrothgar. I will fight with you not only because I am a Scylding but because I have a private account to settle.'

'I respect your offer, Prince, but I cannot accept your help.' His tone was pleasant but there was a lightness about it which showed he did not regard Hrethric seriously. 'I have vowed to stand alone against this monster, Grendel, and if my duguth are stupid with wine, so much the better; they cannot interfere. I have also vowed to fight without helmet, or sword, or shield, or precious corslet.' Angrily he threw the fumbling Hondscio aside and pulled off the ringed armour. His chest and shoulders shaped the tunic's soft cloth. 'I shall take your monster in my arms. I shall hold him in the grasp of my hands which have the strength of thirty men. I shall wrestle with him, thigh against thigh, chest against chest, throw him here upon this floor and bend back his spine until it cracks under my weight.'

'May it be as you say. May the fight be quick, your power greater than that of your adversary and his defeat speedy and complete. Otherwise you, too, may catch the sickness.' Angenga's voice was low and Beowulf strained for the words.

'Sickness, Scop? What sickness is this? Do not riddle with me.' His arms were folded, his feet astride. Charmed by the fight he had described, his eyes were on the doors by which Grendel would enter. He was already the conqueror.

'It is no riddle. It is plain for all to see. I talk of the sickness of fear.'

'Fear?' Beowulf repeated. 'Fear?'

Then he began to laugh. He threw back his head and the noise burst from his wide mouth, swept down the hall and rose to the rafters. It passed through the walls and reached the huts and apartments of the Scyldings who listened in amazement to a sound which for twelve winters had never in the darkness issued out of Heorot. It broke into the ears of his drowsing companions who started up and, uncomprehending but obedient, added their clamour. Discordant and meaningless, their shrieks were a wine-soaked descant to their leader's deeper swell, and together the disbelieving laughter and the inane din grazed past Angenga and Hrethric at the doors and rushed down the avenue of trees.

The strange vibrations radiated across the heathlands, penetrated the fens and marshes, and Grendel, moodily picking over the bones of Oslaf, raised his head.

# SIX

Leading the scop, Hrethric stopped at the door of his own chamber. The laughter from which they had fled was finished and the only sound now was their scratching breath. Around them, the apartments of the court were lapped by the incoming night. Above them, the grey sky was thickening to black. Nothing had shape or edge; shadows and solid things merged and discouraged searching touch, but from one deep fold something crept. It was moist and piteous, a whimper out of a corner, squeezed through nightmare's choking cloths.

'What is that?' Angenga asked.

'It is my brother, Hrothmund. One of the women will give him a potion.'

Lost, seeking comfort, the noise rubbed against them. 'I cannot stay here,' the man said.

'This is my chamber. Won't you stay with me?' Inside, his bed was again heaped with extra furs and many hours must pass before the dawn he longed for.

'Not here, unless I knew that my staying could ease him.' Angenga shivered as the cry momentarily sharpened. 'You must excuse me, Prince. Also, my chamber is better placed to watch for the man-beast.'

'You intend to keep watch?'

'It is part of my profession to observe. My hand dare not wag a sword in the face of Grendel, but at least my eyes and ears will still serve me,' he answered wryly. 'It is a little thing, compared with the other.'

Hrethric did not agree but he said, 'Then I will come with you.'

The night closed behind them as they walked. In the court chambers and in the huts of retainers and craftsmen, all were still. No floorboard creaked under a man's step. No cup jingled upon a trestle. No breath rose from heads heavy upon bolsters. No child whined for milk. Neither dogs who flattened themselves under benches nor horses who huddled in their stalls moved or made sound. It was like a place deserted and not even a wolf howled.

So, brushing against a thing covered in a smooth pelt, Hrethric shrieked before a hand found his mouth. 'Hush, it is me,' Freawaru urged.

'You?' They clutched together. 'You shouldn't be here, startling me. He may have heard.'

'Surely you should not be here alone,' Angenga rebuked softly.

'I wait.'

'You wait? Here?' They were standing under the eaves of her apartment. Behind her, the door was closed.

'I've told you: I am waiting.' In the darkness they felt her turn as if she dismissed them.

'But, Freawaru, he might smell you here. For once he might be attracted away from the hall and come here.'

'Yes.'

They were silenced by her intention, then Hrethric, horrified, burst out, 'Freawaru, you cannot! You must not!'

Angenga stepped to her side and argued, 'It would make no difference, Princess. Even if he tracked you down and he – he took you, he would still plunder Heorot.'

'You cannot be certain. He might not. I say he would

55

not! He must not!' Her voice was shrill.

'Be quiet! He will hear us. She is bringing the monster to us.' Hrethric appealed to the scop, but in one corner of his mind unblurred by panic there was admiration for his sister. Around them, the chambers remained quiet. His first cry of shock and her screeching insistence had roused no one to enquiry. 'Please, Freawaru,' he begged more gently.

'You go. Leave me.' He heard her step forward, saw the darkness lit for a second by white streaks as arms were raised to pummel him, then they disappeared in a bundle against the scop's chest.

'You are coming with us,' Angenga stated, and holding her in a firm embrace, with her mantle dragging at his ankles, he felt his way to his own chamber.

'No, you must not light a taper. It is not permitted during the night of waiting,' Hrethric whispered as he heard the scratch of flint. Somewhere on the floor Freawaru was crying.

'Who does not permit it?' the man snapped. 'A flame would not guide the creature here. It is a thing that requires darkness.' But the sound of the flint ceased and his voice stroked among woollen cloths and furs, over bolsters and through looped hair as he comforted the girl.

'No more tears. They will blotch your pretty face. You are brave, Freawaru, but your mother and father would not wish you to stand at your door alone. They would have commanded me to bring you away. They will need you when your body has grown to match your spirit. How many winters are you? Fourteen? No,' he answered words made indistinct by sobs, 'I do not criticize you. Love is not a subject for reproach.'

The murmurs continued, becoming rhythmic as the scop

56

recited songs to the girl until her weeping diminished and she snuggled into the furs of the bed, ready for sleep. As Angenga drew her mantle over her shoulders, she asked, 'Will Ingeld be a man like the Geat, Scop?'

'Of course. He promises to be very like him,' he replied without hesitation. 'His tribe are mighty warriors.'

'Ah,' she breathed, pleased, and immediately slept.

'Why Ingeld? Why does she ask about Ingeld, a prince of the Heathobards?'

'Because my father has promised her to him. It is a mark of friendship to secure peace with his tribe.' He was afraid of their words rustling the silence.

'Ingeld may doubt the friendship of a king who slew his father Froda.'

'The king Froda killed my father's father, yet Hrothgar offers his daughter to Froda's son,' he answered briefly, still trying to discourage talk.

'And do you believe that the marriage will bring peace? Does your father believe that? This is a matter of king for king, kinsman for kinsman. In such feuds men do not desire peace except as a time for testing and gathering strength. They desire blood. You, a Scylding, know that! Blood spilt for blood spilt: a carcass whitening as the blood drains from the hacked limbs, stripped of its armour, left naked for the raven and wolf to desecrate until only the bones lie under the sun which cracks and crumbles them into dust. And the dust blows through the dust of those other bones, of that other carcass whose blood flowed away under the sword once held in the hand that has become the new dust. There is no end to this, Hrethric. I have witnessed it on other islands, in other kingdoms. Now that Ingeld is grown to manhood, he will seek to avenge the slaughter of his father as surely as Hrothgar repaid the slaughter of his father upon Froda. This girl will be a hostage until that time comes.'

'It is necessary. My father no longer desires war. He hopes that the marriage will prevent it, though my mother cannot believe that and fears for Freawaru in the Heathobard court. But Freawaru is a Scylding, granddaughter of Healfdene whom Froda slew, and she must play her part. If it fails, it will be as fate judges and we shall be ready to carry out its will.'

'Yes; our destiny is already determined,' the scop agreed. 'We cannot step from the path prepared for us even if we guess its goal, as your mother guesses when she looks at Freawaru. But her daughter will not disgrace her. Destiny cannot be conquered but can be met square, without flinch. We must agree but never acquiesce.'

They were silent; and the prince thought of his cousin Hrothulf whose name was like the point of a scramasax against his skull. But if fate willed his death, he resolved, squatting on the floor of the scop's chamber, that he would first blunt the shaft of that scramasax upon his cousin's bones.

Freawaru stirred and a quick sound suggesting laughter reached them.

'She sleeps like a child,' Angenga said. 'I am glad that I told her the Heathobard prince resembles the Beowulf she has tricked out with a girl's fancies, for though I condemn deceits, that lie will support her with hope in the years before her marriage. Do not we owe her a little gladness?'

'You did right,' the other reassured him. 'And you know a great deal about our people and the tribes opposite our coasts.'

'Yes. Like Beowulf, I had heard that Unferth had

murdered a kinsman, but I did not know he was given so much licence in your court.'

'He has many followers and Hrothulf pleaded for him.' Hrethric could say no more. Further comment might be treacherous to his father.

'You must excuse a bard's curiosity. It is a habit and not always acceptable. You say I know a great deal about the tribes. That is true; I have learnt much during my wanderings. There are merchants, adventurers, soldiers, exiles like myself, all men who seek the fellowship of talk after their journeys, always willing to exchange tales of their homelands for a new song. It was a Swede trading furs and amber from the region of Uppsala that told me of the Geats who live to the south of their nation; and of Beowulf and Breca.'

'Do you believe Beowulf's account of their venture? Did he really fight those sea monsters as he said?' He had been mesmerized by the man's story. Now suddenly it was essential that it was true.

'I believe the essence of it. The details are irrelevant. What matters is the man's fearlessness in the face of attackers. I do not doubt that. When I saw the Geat troop marching this morning, I did not suspect that I was observing a warrior out of that trader's story. Now I see him as he is, not through the eyes of another, and have the opportunity to form my own judgement.'

'You will sing of him?'

'I have no choice. I must sing of him, and of this night.'

This night. Hrethric's brain jerked. Sour mucus pumped up his throat then slid back. Splayed out on the floor, his hands were impressed with the pattern of notch and groove. A draught squeezed between the boards, pricking his flesh like the tips of Grendel's nails.

'He is nearer, Angenga. He will hear us. We must not talk.'

'Do not tell me I must not talk. You may deny me light but not speech. That is a comfort and should be passed round like a wine cup among friends. Words are my sword, but tonight they are my armour. Did you not forget the monster while we talked?'

That was true, but the man's speech was hurried and nervous.

'Are you afraid, Angenga?'

'I am afraid. This court is like a place cursed. I do not belong to it; it is not mine. Yet I cannot remain indifferent. I feel my body infected with its canker.' He was shuffling over the floor, tapping with his fingers along the walls, until Hrethric heard him scrabbling with the latch which he had jammed so firmly in its place.

'Do not open the door, Angenga. Please.'

'You think this flimsy barrier would hold back Grendel, if he chose to enter, when the great doors of Heorot are not proof against him?'

'No; it is not for that.' His jaws, his gums, his tongue were now muzzled with cold, but already it was changing. The moment was coming sooner than he expected. 'Come away, Angenga. Do not open it,' he gabbled, his voice rising.

But the latch had snapped up. The door opened back, and as it did so, the scop cried out.

'He is almost upon us,' the young man groaned. 'This is what the monster brings.'

'It seeps out of the earth.'

'This comes ahead of him. First the ice, then this. By it we know that he is close.'

There was no light. Nothing around them was visible. Yet the darkness was marbled with vapours which scurried and eddied, wrapped around them, blew through the night until the air was curdled. And this air, black and spiked with frost, was separated into thin whey. It mixed with the sweat of their skin and dropped gobbets which congealed like grease on their hands.

'This is a fiend's spittle.' Angenga retched with disgust.

'Yes. Let us close the door.'

'I must watch and listen.'

'But you can see nothing!'

'I know where Heorot stands. Stretched between earth and sky, it waits. Inside it a man waits also, balances himself upon the ground which bears the weight of the walls round him, and he strains on tiptoe, upwards, as the gables above him reach up through the mists. I cannot stay behind a door on such a night.' His craft compelled him like an obsessive love. 'Come; come and shelter against me,' he said more kindly.

Hrethric scrambled from his corner and squatted by the man's side.

'You tremble.' Angenga unfastened the brooch at his throat and lifted his cloak over Hrethric's shoulders. So the prince shared the exile's mantle and his body received his warmth.

Together they crouched by the open door. Behind them, Freawaru slept. In front was the knoll topped by the silent Heorot, but neither the curve of the ground nor the hall's lofty bulk was revealed to them. They sat, their ears straining for a sound, their eyes peering for movement. Neither spoke.

Then the night of waiting began to close around

Hrethric. The darkness, fanged with ice, bit through his covering of fur; it tightened over his head; creatures spawned in its breath and crawled over his skin; and its rancid fumes entered his mouth and lodged like a swab in his throat. He was stifled; his arms were pinned to his sides; his mind spun.

He heard his name whispered and felt a hand touch his cheek. 'What is it, Hrethric?'

'Do you not feel it? He is here.'

'I can see nothing.'

'No; we do not see. Do you not feel his grip, his breath?'

The scop gasped and pulled him against his chest. 'There is no one here, my friend.'

But Angenga's voice was overtaken by that of another.

From the deep belly of Heorot, through the portals still rocking from the crack of a demon's fist, a cry leapt out. Wordless, it ululated above the mists, dipped to a creaking groan, then lifted again and grew into a crescendo of squeals that followed one upon another, ever higher, ever sharper, rupturing the throat. Until it was suddenly nipped tight, the remaining breath hissed for a moment, and Heorot was still.

Their ears ringing, the scop and Hrethric cowered under the mantle. Each believed that Beowulf was dead.

But gradually other sounds reached them. At first they were indistinct, sensed rather than heard. For they felt a tremor under the ground, spreading from the base of Heorot and rippling down the knoll as the foundations of the hall quivered under the stress of two massive weights. These advanced towards each other; the floor of the hall shook, then the earth shuddered as the two forces met. For a second they sucked apart like two mighty currents which, colliding headlong, recoil from the impact of each other's thrust. Then they were clamped together; feet thudded, and the listeners knew that Beowulf wrestled with the monster Grendel.

The night, heavy with darkness, throbbed to their fight. Shoulders knocked against walls; feet drummed on the floor; bodies locked together, lunged into pillars, tripped over bolsters, tossed and rolled among the hearth's cold embers. The court, listening, knew the mists of the night were frothed by the turmoil of the fighters' circling and grappling, and all felt the strain of muscles, of backs braced against wrenching arms.

And Heorot, so often spattered with blood, was ripped and bruised. Taut floorboards cracked as a body was thrown down; another, hurled against the doors, bent the gleaming hinges; carved benches, kicked aside, shattered against the posts; smooth tables reared, smashed down, and their tight joints burst; silver goblets spun into corners and were dented against discarded armour; golden cups were crunched under pounding feet. No sound came from the mouths of the wrestlers but in the clank of precious metal and the slit of chiselled wood, the hall mourned.

Huddled under the scop's cloak, Hrethric and his friend looked into the night. The vapours foamed round them, covering their faces with glutinous slime which added to the sweat starting from their pores at every sound that thundered through the walls of Heorot. To each one they gave a movement: the crash of a trestle meant two bodies sprawled among jutting splinters; the ring of metal showed them golden cups scattered as the fighters scrambled to their feet. Hearing timbers echo, they imagined a head battered against a wall; by a thud they knew that one was tossed upon the boards, that he was pinned down by grinding knees, that hands were knotted over his throat; and as benches cracked apart they saw the assailant thrown off, flung among the wooden seats which skidded and broke under his weight, and they knew that he would leap up, mouth set, his arms outstretched, stalking his prey. Then they would join again, arms hooped round arched backs, squeezing into ribs and pressing chest against chest, thigh against thigh.

All this Angenga and the prince guessed as they followed the course of the struggle. Their muscles ached. Their limbs grew weary. Their minds were numbed by the contest, and their bodies froze in the night's rank mists.

Then, around them the grip of the dark began to slacken. The air swayed as if a breeze, far off, were stirring the borders of the night, and a new sound lifted from the wreck of seats and trestles. At first it was no more than a breath rattling painfully from a dry throat but gradually it grew louder, swelled upward and, forced from the bellows of giant lungs, a howl burst forth. It buffeted the rafters, beat against the gables, tore through the thatch and soared into the sky. Discordant, tuneless, it was a baying wild with frustration and clenched with pain, the agony of one who was mastered but who strove against that mastery with notes that bucked and plunged. And even as his anguish tolled over the court, the listeners trembled at the fury which only death would subdue.

The cry continued, became a knell whose melody spoke of sinews cruelly ripped, of blood boiling from split veins. Harsh and awesome, the threnody went on, but his voice grew weaker; his strength diminished; his power fled away; and at last the bonds of frost loosened and the mists began to part.

So, watching, Hrethric and the scop saw a mass push from the doors of Heorot. More black than the thinning night, it stumbled down the avenue, a creature tormented with pain and humiliation, desperate to lick his wound and snatch his last breaths among the litter of his secluded lair. And as the wailing receded and was sucked into the marshes, the first light of a new day showed at last through the trees.

## SEVEN

The dawn slowly drifted through the broken doors
of Heorot. Inch by inch its light spread along the floor,
sank into gouged posts, sifted through gaping timbers and
climbed over trampled bolsters and fractured planks, once
benches and trestles, which sloped in random heaps like
things driven by blast. As the light fanned out and crept
among the rubble of the two outer aisles, it touched bundles
of cloth pressed against the walls; they were mantles and
tunics pulled tight over the bodies of men, and they
took the shape of knees drawn up to protect or of limbs
contorted in fear.

There was one, however, who neither hid nor groaned.
He stood by the hearth, towering above the ruin caused by
his night's labours, and he did not turn at the sound of
the watchers' steps. Hrethric and his friend stopped and
regarded him.

Alone and silent he stared at the charred logs at his feet.
The flames had wilted at the coming of the demon; the
logs had dripped flakes of grey ash during the combat and
now, still and brooding, the man leant over the cold hearth
stones as if waiting for fire to kindle the dead embers and
the fire of his own spirit to be renewed. For he was very
weary. His shoulders stooped; his arms hung slack and heavy;
the muscles were flaccid in his calves; his feet did not arch
but were flattened upon the floor; his hair was matted with
sweat which still ran from his neck, streamed down the

66

trough between the muscles of his shoulders and spread over his back. This, turned towards them, still heaved as his lungs strove for breath and was disfigured with the marks of his adversary. There was no blood, but his skin was rashed with scratches from a rough hide or needling bristles and at his waist was the livid stamp of huge hands bordered with the impression of pointed claws.

So, with muscles spent and flesh bruised, the warrior looked into the dead fire and waited. Like a creature maimed in a fight who crawls away from the pack to nurse his wound, Beowulf kept his back turned, preferring to nurse his frailty in private until it was replaced by new strength. He did not greet the prince and Angenga, nor did his posture change when, along the sides of the hall, stiff limbs were stretched, cloaks were turned back, and his troop began to scramble through the debris of the night. But the rocking planks which tripped them, the crushed goblets which clanked at their heels, the print of the man-beast's brand on their leader's flesh, all these were less real to them than the horror which still stalked through their minds. They had lain down fuddled by wine yet their senses had not been numbed by its fumes and their night had not been blank of terrors.

They huddled together in the centre of the hall, their eyes flicking from their leader to the wide avenue now clearly visible beyond the wrecked doors, until suddenly they were aware of something odd about the composition of their group. Agitated, they looked round the circle, each man searching for the same face, then, not finding it, they sprang apart as if they had no right to share companionship and warmth. Because their thoughts had struggled back through the din of the fight and they had heard again that first scream. At its memory, many covered their eyes, but one stared, appalled, at a scrap of cloth he found in his grasp and lurched away until he came to Hrethric and the scop.

'It was here! Over me. A stench. Sludge, vomit, carcasses rotting,' the man choked out, clutching the scop's arm. 'Its eyes. They were red, glowing, never a blink. You could see by them. They found Hondscio, not me – Hondscio. I saw him red in the beams from those eyes. He twisted about. His mouth was open. It was black, screaming. Blood bubbled through the rings of his corslet. There was a bag, a pouch, swaying from the monster's wrist. It was scabby with dried blood and rattled, as if full of bones. Hondscio was pulled up. His legs were kicking. But the screaming stopped because there was a crunch, then more. I heard it. I heard him mashed, sucked.' The man paused, then moaned, 'And I did not stop it.'

'You tried, my friend,' Angenga attempted to give comfort, though the hand that supported the Geat shook and his face was white. 'See, you have a fragment of his tunic. That shows that you tried to pull Hondscio away.'

'I do not remember. The monster leant over me. I was stifled by the stale grease on his belly. I could do nothing. I believe that he ripped off Hondscio's corslet and stuffed it into his bag. Perhaps his tunic, too, and this piece fell. I had drunk much and though my sword was at my side, it remained in its scabbard. Our leader avenged his death but I do not think I tried to prevent it,' he insisted dismally.

'You did something,' Angenga repeated. 'Do not accuse yourself so harshly. Hondscio did not die forsaken by his friend.'

'The scop is right. You are a warrior and did all that

friends would hope to do,' Hrethric said, his eyes on the shred of fabric in the man's hand. After that other night of waiting, if he had held a piece of Oslaf's tunic, he believed that his soul would be easier now; but his hands were empty and it was too late to treasure a wisp of cloth inside his palm.

'Perhaps,' the Geat half conceded, but the talk had calmed him. He folded the cloth and pushed it into the sheath of his scramasax, flat and safe against the blade. For a moment he was quiet, revering his friend, then he turned upon Hrethric and his face was tight with reproach. 'You speak of warriors and friendship. What do you Scyldings know of that, you who cannot avenge your own duguth but must wait for a man from another kingdom to rid you of your curse? Hondscio is dead, dead because he came to aid you. Our king did not wish this venture. He and his counsellors considered that the Scyldings should be left to settle their own matters, but Beowulf insisted because of the ties between his father and yours. So we came with him, out of fellowship and love. We knew the risks. We did not expect that all of us would return to our homeland. But do not think that when Hondscio died, he died for the Scyldings. He did not sacrifice his life for your people but in love and loyalty to his Geat lord.'

Shocked, Hrethric tried to find an answer, but his stutters were interrupted.

Beowulf had swung round from the hearth. With feet planted wide apart he faced down the aisle towards the light. He glanced at Angenga and the prince, then regarded his followers. Neither by one brief wince nor by a few sorrowing words did he acknowledge that one was not with them. Instead, his eyes commanded them to shed weakness and fear. Until gradually under his gaze their backs straightened; their cheeks lost the grey and were coloured with health; breathing in his vigour, they became again a band of fighters who were alert and flexed. Still he said nothing, but, as the need to strengthen them was removed, his face changed. A frown channelled the skin on his forehead; his nostrils widened; his jaws clenched, grinding his teeth. Swinging to and fro over the wreckage of the hall, his eyes glared, until finally his fury exploded.

He lifted his head and with a noise that shook the rafters, bellowed, 'I could not stay him! I had him clamped to my side but I could not stay him! We were matched to the weight of a hair, and he could not crush me nor could I crack his ribs and squeeze the breath from his lungs. He was vile, slippery with filth and sleeked with the fat of stinking carrion but his skill was beyond measure. His hands were like icicles and stuck to my flesh; his legs were iron bands round my thighs. Never on this earth have I met such a wrestler and never in the regions that he inhabits had he found a contestant as powerful as I. He was a creature, loathsome, spewed out of stagnant bogs and yet I could not throttle him in this grip which has the pressure of thirty men!'

He was stamping; his fists pawed the air; his teeth gnashed, and the hall rocked at the blast of his trumpeting wrath. 'So we grappled. Neither gave ground, but each knew that the other was pitched to the topmost of his strength. I was bound by his embrace; these arms pinioned his foul body to my naked chest, and as we rolled upon this floor we knew that our force was equal and that neither of us could increase his grip. Until, suddenly, as we struggled for another hold, my hands linked round his upper arm. I heard him gasp and I knew at last that my power would triumph. He pulled away, slewed round, pushed his scaled palm in my face and did not shrink when my teeth met his flesh, but he could not clasp me. His other arm was useless. My hands were fastened over it, bending it into his back. My whole weight pressed upon him and yet he would not crumble! He would not sink his belly upon this floor!'

Again Beowulf stamped, beating out his anger. 'He jerked and twisted. My grip held. His flesh swelled up between my fingers and he yelped with the pain. Then, with my hands still latched round his arm, he tried to fly from this hall, dragging me with him across the floor until my feet found a purchase against the base of a post and I wrenched him back. And the muscles of his arm stretched further and snapped; the skin ripped open at the shoulder; the bone tore from its socket; sinews and veins split; blood spurted and he fell away, stumbled away from me, with the bone jutting from the hole at his shoulder and the ribs curving through his open side. That wound is mortal, but he escaped from me! He escaped from my grasp!' Fierce with chagrin, he spat out the words. 'I did not stay him. He is gone, leaving me with this, nothing but this as a trophy for my pains.'

He bent down, caught up something from the mess by the hearth and swung it above his head. At the sight of it his listeners fell back. For it was an arm, stippled with a shag of hair which stood in spikes through crusting blood. Held at the wrist, the hand was screwed in the convulsion of pain and plucked at the air which whistled between the stiff bent fingers as Beowulf whirled the arm round, round, a dark, dead arm extended from his own which was glossy and powered with flicking muscle. The limb of the monster thrashed under the roof of Heorot; the swish of its circling passage scattered the dust which hovered in the day's light and from its torn extremity, strips of frayed skin, twisted thongs of sinews and the ragged cords of dried blood streamed out like crimson pennants in the draught.

Beowulf continued to shout. 'I had him against my breast. He was mine! He knew it. I had conquered him, but he would not submit. He would not die here, in this hall, where he had prowled bloated with slaughter. Honour was unknown to him; he would not stay on the battlefield until taken by death, but neither would he leave it whole and victorious. So he ripped himself from me. Our strength, his and mine, gave him a wound which will kill him. Yet still he cheated me of his carcass. His wretched body, sagging as the life poured from the crater at his shoulder, slipped from my grip, leaving me with this. Only this! It should be his carcass I heave above my head!'

Then suddenly his ranting ceased. His body tensed. For a few more seconds the arm whipped round, then it was released, spun down the aisle, crashed against the jamb of the doorway, slid down, and through a spurt of splinters and dust, settled on the threshold like a crooked branch. Only inches behind it, a figure stood against the light.

'Take the spoil of battle, Scylding,' the warrior boomed. 'It belongs to your people. I surrender it without regret.'

With a movement expressing revulsion, Unferth poked the limb with a supple foot. 'An unusual trophy,' he commented, 'but I may be wrong; I have never practised wrestling. Perhaps if you renounce the subtleties of the blade and rely on brawn, you must risk leaving hunks of yourself as battle prizes instead of more elegant armour. One could argue that we should count ourselves fortunate that this is all we are left with, for the question arises what we are to do with it.'

'The answer is simple. We will hang it on your wall, just as you would hang any other trophy from the field of combat.' Gesturing to his troop, he commanded, 'Take up the monster's scrag and leash it to the outer gables.' At which one sprang forward and, followed by his companions, bore it through the doors.

'So you have carried out your boast,' Unferth continued. Seeing the arm, he had not permitted himself to betray shock or awe and now he withheld compliment. Hrethric was astonished at his discourtesy until he remembered that only he and the scop were witness to it. 'It will be a story to enthral the Geat court, whom we know love such pieces, and I wager that their taste for sensation will not be disappointed, since no doubt it will be more than the demon's arm you will have ripped off by the time you recount the exploit. Fate has cast for you, Geat traveller, for it is not often that a man discovers such a conclusive way of clearing his character after a misspent youth.'

'You refer again to Breca? That has already been explained. Your hints are like the smear of a child's thumb on a warrior's sword. They cannot tarnish me, Scylding.' But his chin was thrust out and there was a slight flush in his cheek.

'Oh, I'm not thinking only of Breca. There have been other rumours.' Unferth shrugged. 'But what is rumour, after all? No more than gossip distorted by the tongues which pass it along its course. I spoke merely to reassure you that, however unjustly valued in your youth, you will now receive suitable acclaim. Whatever you think of the Scyldings, you must admit that we gave you a chance to save your reputation.'

'That was never at stake. What I have saved is your kingdom, Counsellor,' Beowulf snapped. His hand had crossed to his side where no sword hung. It was clear that the other's taunts had scratched a nerve. They faced each other: the Geat massive, half naked, the hairs on his body blunt with dried sweat, and the Scylding lean, dapper in fresh tunic and mantle, sharp as a barb.

'You are clever, Scylding, but your cleverness sleeps when you talk of my youth or when you encourage your henchmen to force treacherous wine upon my men until they are defenceless. Such things are not forgotten, Counsellor.'

Unferth's lips curved in a sneer but he withheld further retort and glided aside as he heard footsteps behind him.

Hrothgar stood under the gables of Heorot, looking up at the lifeless arm. Once it had slit the thick doors over which it hung; once it had groped among his duguth; once companions and warriors, counsellors and friends had been stunned by its weight and had been crumbled like autumn leaves in the press of the sinews now drooping in tatters from the wound. But there was no gloating on the king's face when he gazed upon the desperate payment of his enemy; there was no exclamation of triumph. Only a frown of pain nipped his forehead as he remembered his dead. Then he entered the hall, his face solemn but no longer gaunt, his hair burnished to silver in the caress of the early sun, his jewelled clasps glinting out from the curls of his white fur mantle; and his hands were free, not resting upon the arm of Wealhtheow and Hrothulf beside him, and his step was brisk, compelling a quick pace from Freawaru who followed and from retainers who carried goblets and jugs of wine.

'So, you have expelled him, Beowulf, son of Ecgtheow,' he greeted, emphasizing each word. 'I and my people bow to you in reverence and gladness. Your courage will be a leaping flame which guides my duguth through the dust of battle, your name a precious gem in the hilt of their swords. Your combat this night will be for ever honoured by my people and your fame will be known throughout the regions of the earth.'

'You are generous, Hrothgar, King of the Scyldings, but my aim was to carry out my promise. I had no other ambition.'

'And that you have done. You have purged my Heorot of evil; you have cast out the demon, and he will not return. The fogs of the marshlands, the black frost of the fastness will not sustain their creature who returns crippled by a power greater than his. They will not stanch his wound, and already that instrument of his greed and malice shrivels under the day's sun. Together with its fellow it rubbed against your shoulders; its bristles combed through the down at your throat and its nails dimpled your skin, but it could not harm you, Beowulf; it could not enter your flesh. The pinch of the demon was here, my friend, but see, the bruises shrink, for tissue and vein withstood the monster's grasp. Yet I suspect they were sorely tried,' and stretching out, Hrothgar traced his finger along the weals striping a shoulder and round the mottled bars at the waist.

Beowulf remained still, wooed by the king's gentleness. 'He fought well. There were times when my body was weak as a woman's. It was hard then not to surrender,' he confessed in a low voice.

'I understand,' the king sighed back, 'but we must not be ashamed of our bodies' frailty. If the spirit holds firm, it will support the weakness of our flesh, as yours did. So we confront the enemy and do not cower before the will of fate. Ecgtheow, your father, would have had great joy in his son's deed, and it is not only to honour you for subduing the monster that I wish to do one thing this day, but also in memory of your father's loyalty and love when I sheltered him in this hall.'

Hrothgar paused. His eyes glanced over the queen and Freawaru, smiled at Hrethric, settled for a moment on the faces of his nephew and Unferth and lingered on the wrinkled face of Aeschere as if seeking from his oldest friend and most trusted counsellor an approval for what he was about to say.

'Beowulf, warrior of the Geats, grandson of Hrethel and nephew of their king, Hygelac,' he crooned the words with tenderness and affection, 'I, Hrothgar, King of the Scyldings, would take you as my son.'

A rustle passed through the group. Hrothulf made a step forward. Unferth's expression was wary and calculating. Hrothgar ignored them all. His hands were stretched out, cupped to receive the touch of the Geat's huge palm.

'You honour me beyond what I deserve. I will be a son to you in all ways that are in my power,' Beowulf answered, his face serious and his clasp steady.

'May the deity bless our linked hands this day. But I keep you from rest. Aeschere will conduct you to your chamber. Even a wrestler such as you requires sleep and refreshment after labour.' The king was merry now. 'Yet first we will drink a cup of wine, to slake your thirst a little and to pledge our words.'

Surrounded by the chief persons in the Scylding court, Beowulf drank from the cup which Freawaru shyly brought to him, swallowing the wine hastily like a man indifferent to its flavour. When the others raised their goblets to him, he gave a quick impatient nod and stared without expression at Unferth standing close to the nephew of the king. 'You must excuse me, my lord. My limbs are heavy.'

'Yes. We will not delay you further, my son. When you are rested we will feast to celebrate your victory and our release.' Taking Beowulf's goblet, he handed it to a retainer, at the same time declining more wine for himself. 'Once again the night will receive the sound of our banquet. Darkness will nestle content under our eaves; it will curl in slumber at the base of these walls, and it will warm itself in the light from these doors. The song of our pleasure will ride upon the night's breezes, blowing before it the steam of the marshes which will cool and sprinkle the earth with healing drops of clear dew. And Heorot, my Heorot, which I built to gladden the eyes of men with beauty, this Heorot, now desolate and wounded, shall be renewed. Its walls shall be repaired; new hinges shall be forged; benches and tables shall be replaced, and the silken banners of the hosts of the Scyldings shall be hung from the rafters and flutter in the draughts of our joy.'

Hrothgar turned and, followed by his retinue and Beowulf, walked out of the hall and into the morning sun.

Under its brittle light the knoll was rippled with movement. Retainers scurried between the huts; cooks heaved buckets from the stream and ran back with water licking against their calves; farmers strode down the tracks hustling sheep before them or prodding reluctant pigs with goads; a group of fowlers, hooped with slender bows and circled by dogs, was already pushing through the bushes fringing the wood; and the sons of smiths and joiners

77

carried baskets of charcoal and planks of seasoned wood to the huts where the craftsmen hammered and welded, chopped and chiselled, starring the air with sparks of metal, hazing it with the blond dust of wood and motes of curled shavings, and festooning the thatch of their huts with smoke. While among the chambers of the court, duguth and counsellors walked briskly, called out orders, laid out ceremonial armour and rode to welcome thanes from outlying settlements. For the news of Grendel's defeat had run swifter than the dawn over Hrothgar's kingdom and men had set out to see the wonder that he had left behind him and the first of them were already appearing along the lower paths.

They came, thanes and churls, farmers and fishermen, old warriors and young men hoping one day to serve among the geogoth. Some walked with long untiring steps, others sat high on cantering horses, and all faces were set towards the avenue, impatient for the moment when they would turn into it and see, at its crest, the arm of the monster knotted upon the wall.

'It is a magnificent trophy. This hanging arm justifies Beowulf's boast,' the scop said to Hrethric.

'Your praise is too reserved, Angenga.' Below them he could see Freawaru, an empty dish in her hands, latching the door of Beowulf's chamber behind her. It was an office he wished he could perform himself. 'Have you ever heard of anything that can compare with what Beowulf has done?'

'No; I have not. I shall make a lay that will be all your admiration demands.'

A lump of peeled gristle, slipping from the beak of the raven pecking above them, dropped at the scop's feet. Bending down, he scooped up dust and let it sift between his fingers until the piece of flesh was hidden from curious eyes. 'Do not criticize a traveller's sentiment, though this death was deserved,' he said, defying Hrethric's frown.

'He was our enemy. We owe him no burial.' But he controlled the impulse to kick aside the little heap of dust.

All around him the air was clean. The sun twinkled through the branches laced across the avenue down which the visitors were now advancing, their faces already shocked at the thing which waited at the end of their path; but not one of them blenched as his feet cracked the brown scabs which had dried over the gouts of the monster's blood. On either side of them the knoll was quickened with energy and purpose and the slight, crisping wind was fluting with unaccustomed song. There was no comparable morning in Hrethric's memory.

'Come, Angenga, there is much to do. We must attend upon my mother.' He spoke urgently, trying to dispel the melancholy sobering the man's face. 'No doubt she will have tasks for us. You know the way of women. Perhaps she will wish to hear what lays you can perform. You may even have to give a rehearsal before all that gaggle of simpering maidservants. Look, down there some of the geogoth are saddling their mares. They are taking them to the beach to race and sport.' For a moment he thought of the friend he had last raced with, whose horse remained unsaddled in its stall, but, 'Perhaps I shall join them and you will come with us; the winds from the sea will freshen your lungs. And see, there is the priest with a group of thanes going to the shrine to offer sacrifices of thanks to the deity; and there is Aeschere, walking so fast that those thanes can hardly keep up with him, so fast you cannot believe he is crippled with rheumatism and a wound in the shoulder that took the sword thrust meant for my father in a war long ago. He and the others are making for the closed chamber where the Scylding treasure is stored. Aeschere will choose the gifts that Beowulf will receive from my father tonight.'

Then his chatter stopped for Aeschere had halted before a woman; he had spoken, his hands upon hers, his worn frame bent over her in an attitude of protection and pity. The woman was Oslaf's mother.

'Beowulf has done what we failed to do. He has done what many of us did not dare. He has avenged those who died. I wish I could have been as fearless as he.'

'To fight without fear commands respect, but to fight when our limbs are cramped with terror and our bowels are knotted with dread, that is the greater courage. I believe that Beowulf has yet to learn that, Hrethric, whereas you know the necessity and I think that you will not evade the fight when it comes.'

He was echoing something of the king's words to Beowulf but the young man scarcely listened. This scop and his father were old and cautious whereas the Geat was daring, laughing at danger, his limbs moulded for battle, a warrior in his prime. 'He has no blemish. He is a model for us all. I am proud to receive him as a brother.'

'Your words make mine appear ungracious,' Angenga conceded but he could not prevent a sigh. 'It is a good thing that you approve of your father's decision. Let us hope that no bad consequences come of it.'

'Are you questioning my father's wisdom?' the other demanded angrily.

'Your reproach is just. I overstep what is permitted to a stranger.'

Across the knoll retainers who had accompanied

Aeschere were carrying slim rolls out of the chamber so long undisturbed. As they tied them to cords slung between poles, the brilliant cloth unfurled and the banners of Hrothgar's host which had led his men into battle and brought them undefeated home fluttered in the wind, head high above the grass. So airing in the winter light, they flapped and waved, their golden threads glittering, like great leaves burnt by the sun but not yet ready to fall. And the geogoth who had assembled on their horses whirled about them, formed into laughing ranks behind them, broke, cantered round them, made feints at each other with pretended swords, then whooping and yelling they charged in a jostling group through the court and into the trees. Watching them disappear, Hrethric knew he would not follow. The banners remained, their use laid aside, their beauty now an ornament for a feast, but as they tossed vigorously or pulled taut on the restraining cord, some of their former bravery was revealed to him and he knew that his place was with them.

He turned back to the scop. 'Do not let us quarrel, Angenga. I spoke hastily. Forgive me. Neither of us can foretell the consequences of a deed done today or of a word said. Do not let us spoil this day. Surely you, a voyager, have learnt how to embrace fitful joys.'

'You are right, but I am a poor teacher. An exile's capacity for gladness leaves him as the cliffs of his native coast vanish behind the barrier of waves.'

'What is wrong, my friend? What makes you so sad this day?'

'Yes, today is Beowulf's victory. Heorot is cleansed. The banquet is being prepared. Yet my spirits are heavy. I should not inflict my feelings upon you.'

He paused. The visitors who had come to view Grendel's arm had reached the end of the avenue. They stood at a short distance from the scop and Hrethric, a group of men pushing and nudging, whistling out exclamations, gaping, calling out curses. One picked up a pebble and threw it with a hunter's precise aim. It hit one of the long curved nails and bounced back. Catching it up, the man gave an oath and held the pebble for the rest to see. Its smooth surface was chipped and veined with cracks where it had hit the nail. And immediately a growl rose as if from one huge mouth. Teeth were bared; hands clawed at the soil; and the air was thick with flying stones, grit and dust until the dense hairs and the drooping fist and the raw flesh stuck to the knob of bone were covered with a grey rind. Then the men turned away, seeking friends in the huts of craftsmen or in the rooms of thanes and the raven flapped down again to resume its eating, umindful of the dust.

Angenga said, 'You see, to me it is all one. I give you a riddle: Alone I wander the earth. Cold, hail and tempests are my companions. For fate has set a curse upon me. It has bereft me of my lord, the bright giver of rings. I hear the songs of men in their halls; I smell their feasting and see the light of their fires, but these are denied me. I am an outcast rejected by men. I may not share their gladness, and my mind is set with despair which darkens my deeds. In solitude I must suffer painful death. No one will mourn my going, and all will despise and mock my lonely corpse.'

'Come, Angenga, that is not true. We shelter you. We have befriended you.'

But Hrethric's words were cut short by the man who, looking up at Grendel's arm, answered softly, 'It is not only of myself I speak.'

# EIGHT

The preparations for the banquet were advancing. Inside Heorot retainers were gathering up the broken trestles and benches while new ones were being carried by panting craftsmen up the knoll.

'I must help Aeschere,' Hrethric said. It was true, but it was also necessary for him to get away from his friend's distressed face.

'We are creatures of moods, we poets. They must be borne, for without them there would be no songs,' Angenga apologized and tried to smile.

The gifts had been selected and lay now in Aeschere's chamber, the freshly burnished metal shimmering on a dusky fur. Hrethric ran his fingers along the ridge which protected the helmet's crown, stroked them over the bronze panels inside the iron frame, felt the incised patterns curling and looping across the cheek guards and the crimson garnets set in the moulded curve of the brows. Other garnets winked in the silver pommel of the sword, and the battle banner was a sheet of gold as light fired the woven threads. Beside it, the iron corslet was a heap of luminous rings. These were reflected in the polished blade of the sword which, beaten from welded bands, was a lithe shaft bending under the pressure of Hrethric's slight touch. Down its length the cutting edges were capped with fine ground strips of paler steel. It was an heirloom of his dynasty and, reaching down for it, Hrethric balanced it in his hand.

'No war gear can compare with this,' Aeschere said reverently, including all the gifts. 'The king wishes the warrior to receive no less.'

'He is right. I am glad we have such treasure to give.'

The other nodded, relieved that the prince made no objection. 'Horses, too, are being chosen − eight, the best we have. It is many winters since Hrothgar bestowed gifts in Heorot and I cannot remember any so magnificent. We live again the victories of our youth.' The rheum of age bulged at Aeschere's lower lids, but his speech was vigorous and as he moved to take something from a retainer at the door, his steps were swift. 'And this also Hrothgar wishes Beowulf to possess. I myself will place it on the tallest stallion when it is groomed.'

He held a saddle whose leather shone like bronze and was worked at the border with raised patterns of snakes and was fringed with gold cords. Inlaid with ivory and faceted chips of coloured glass, the wooden saddle-bow arched, proud and commanding. Standing before the old counsellor and his burden, like a worshipper before a priest, Hrethric laid a palm on the bow's crest.

'My father will give this?'

'The king will not ride on this again. Those days are past,' Aeschere replied quietly. 'One as fine will be made for you when your time comes.' He knelt down and, by the side of the staring helmet, placed the saddle which had borne Hrothgar to battle and brought him home triumphant and unharmed.

'I wish my father had not commanded that.' Treasure, heirlooms, horses were Hrothgar's to give as he wished, but this saddle was different and for a moment Hrethric's eyes blurred. To relinquish it seemed like a surrender. It was as if he were not only giving up the saddle but kingship itself, for who but the king led his warriors to fight? From the doorway of Aeschere's chamber the young man could see the ensigns of the victorious Scyldings still beating in the wind; past them, backwards and forwards, thanes and retainers hurried at their tasks. They were the king's subjects, held by bonds of loyalty and service to a monarch who protected them and who, like a father, was responsible for their kin. They would follow where their king led. Hrethric looked down and saw that the sword which was an heirloom of his people still hung from his hand. Raising it to his chest, he drew his finger across the sparkling edge, then with an abrupt movement brushed it against his lips.

'My father chose well,' he said to Aeschere, handing back the sword.

'As he will choose for you one day, my prince,' and Hrethric knew that the old man had seen his gesture. 'And though it would grieve me if I were to outlive my king, I should find some consolation in carrying his sword to his son. But we should not talk of such matters today. I am old, but for twelve winters I have never felt so far from death as I did this dawn. And you – you should be riding with the geogoth. Exercise will increase your hunger and thirst for tonight's feast. Yet I forget. Your mother wishes to speak to you. I must not delay you any longer.'

The sun was directly above him now. Its warmth, though weak and fleeting, gave a hint of the coming spring. Strands of thin steam were drawn upward from the thatch, creamed by smoke which filtered through from the fires beneath. The paths between the chambers were shafts of light straight as the sun's beams, and the earth under Hrethric's feet was no longer sticky with an alien slime but dry and firm. In the apartments either side of him there was whistling and song. Men and women bowed in greeting as he passed and he strode with the warmth of Beowulf's day on his shoulder and the touch of the Scylding sword on his mouth.

The queen's door was half closed, but he could hear her voice and without thinking he pushed forward and entered her chamber. She was standing with her back pressed against one of the wooden pillars, a man's hands on her shoulders. He removed them quickly when he heard Hrethric's step. The man was Hrothulf.

'See, your prince is here, lady. You have powers of divination or very acute ears, Hrethric, to come so promptly when we speak of you.' The man's light tone was a pretence; he was clearly annoyed at the interruption.

'Aeschere said you wished to speak to me,' Hrethric addressed his mother, but he could not look at her.

'Indeed? And what had you to say, Wealhtheow? It must be important if you summon him from the gaiety of the day.'

'It is a personal matter.'

The sun blinded him as Hrethric felt along the door jamb but against its glare remained two figures, forever gripped in the attitude he had witnessed. 'I'll come when you are free, Mother,' stumbling at the name.

'Free!' The intonation was so harsh and unlike her that he swung back. 'Stay, please, Hrethric.'

'Let your mother say what she has to tell you, cousin. It is not so private that it must be kept secret from your husband's nephew, is it, Wealhtheow? Are we not all kin?'

Hrothulf put an arm around the woman and her son felt the blood flushing his cheeks; but, far more than the arm, the man's bantering manner as he presumed the right to listen, demonstrated that he was in control. Wealhtheow neither moved to him nor shrank away and she kept her face empty of expression as she regarded her son.

'I intended to tell him the arrangements for the banquet,' she answered evenly and with a shock Hrethric knew she lied. 'It is his duty to help entertain the warriors. I wish him to sit by the side of Beowulf.'

'Well, there you are, Hrethric. Is not that a pretty touch? Two brothers together. What do you feel about having a new kinsman? I suppose you can only gape in awe – rather undignified but no more than can be expected at your age. Whereas, for your mother to receive that man as a son – that is ludicrous. It insults her youth.' The mockery had become savage.

'I have told you that you strain the point, Hrothulf. It is only a formality.'

'If it is only that, why do you not consent to have it removed?'

'There is nothing I can do.'

'That is untrue. Do not think you can deceive me. It suits Hrothgar's purpose to name Beowulf as his son. The Geat strengthens his failing arm.'

'That was not my lord's reason. He honours the warrior in gratitude and love.'

'Love! The whole court simpers before the Geat. Even Freawaru fawns like a churl. Love! What does Hrothgar know of love?' He was holding her arms, glaring down into her face, snarling with frustration; but as she looked up at him, her lips quivering, he paused. Anger drained from his voice and he finished slowly, leaning on each word. 'Wealhtheow, why does it have to be thus? Why are you not my queen?'

A cough broke the stillness and at the door Unferth said, 'You are required, my lord.'

'You must excuse me, lady.' His friend at his shoulder, Hrothulf paused in the doorway. 'And remember what I have said.'

'It would be impossible to forget,' she murmured as they disappeared across the knoll.

'I must go, Mother.' He did not wish to be alone with her. He had to try to forget the sight of her in Hrothulf's embrace.

Again she prevented him. 'No, stay. I suspect that you judge too hastily, Hrethric.'

'I do not understand. I only know what I have heard and seen.'

'It is time you learnt to see beyond what your eyes show you,' she snapped. 'You would be a man. Is it necessary for me to teach you how to become one? How long must I carry the burden of your youth?'

Stung by the unfair accusation, he answered as he could not have answered before that day. 'I cannot help my youth. I cannot make the years pass more quickly. And I do not ask for your protection. I can look after myself. As for seeing beyond what my eyes show me, I will tell you what I see. I see my father, sitting alone in his chamber, unaware that his love is betrayed.'

He had said it and for a moment the rafters spun round his head, then steadied, and he saw that Wealhtheow had recoiled from him, a hand at her throat.

'You are a most apt pupil. But you are mistaken. I do not betray Hrothgar's trust. Indeed, everything I do is prompted by devotion to him and obligation to the Scylding line.'

'Which includes accepting the attentions of Hrothulf?'

88

'It includes that, too.'

'Why do you let him love you?' He could not stop the words.

'How can I prevent him? Your tongue learns more rapidly than your heart, Hrethric, but some day you will discover that passions are capricious and not subject to men's will. I do not return his feelings; neither can they be entirely dismissed. A man capable of such affection must have within him some good.'

There was no vanity in her claim, though it flattered her, and Hrethric realized that she was talking to him as a man in spite of what she had first said. It was true that he knew nothing of such things but, encouraged, he continued more quietly. 'Yet he desires the throne. We both know that. He wants the throne. Would he have you as his queen?'

'Yes; but that is a different matter.'

'Do you desire that, Mother? Would you be his queen?' He had to know.

'You ask me that? You, the son of the king, ask me whether I imagine that man as my husband while your father still rules his people and shares my bed? I am no churl that insures against the future by licking the hand of a younger lord!' Outraged, disappointed by his clumsy question, she was tense with anger. 'For twelve years, while the monster harried our court, I have been harassed by that man. While the king mourned his duguth, I have kept the peace. Hrothulf desires the throne, yes, he desires it, but not as you think, not as a king succeeding after the other's natural death. He wants it now. He has wanted it for these twelve years. At any price. At the price of Hrothgar's death; at the price of his thanes' slaughter; at the price of the destruction of Heorot; at the price of your murder. Do not look so surprised! Is not his henchman, Unferth, the best adviser on the subject of killing kin?

'All this I know, though naturally he has never dared to confess it, because bound together with all this, like the tails of these two snakes inextricably woven together in this brooch on my breast, is his love for me. I and the throne are one to him. He cannot imagine himself as king without me as his queen. And all this time, had I by one gesture, by one slight, unthinking hint given him cause to believe that I accepted him – Hrothgar, you and the rest of my children would have been dead that day. Yet to prevent that was easy, compared with the other thing I had to do. I could not entirely repulse him for I had to keep him in hope that his ambition would one day be realized, making him wait, as I, too, waited. But I was waiting for something else, watching you, Hrethric, waiting as you grew from child to boy and from boy to young man, hoping that you would reach a man's full strength before your father died, so that you could confront your cousin and claim the throne that is your right.' She paused, her head bowed as if the explanation had exhausted her.

'I never guessed the part you played, Mother. I should not have spoken as I did.'

'He underestimates one thing. Obsessed with the thought of the throne, he does not understand that I would not prefer it, with him, to the lives of husband and children. He cannot enter into a mother's feelings. So, unknown to him, I have a strength and endurance greater than his.' She looked up, and in her eyes was an expression that Hrethric had never seen there before; it was the savagery of a creature at bay, defending her young. 'He shall not have the throne. It is yours. I shall defend your right to the last drop of my blood. And if he or one of his men ever touches you, if your skin is grazed by no more than one scratch of his sword, then I shall take this dagger at my belt and drive it into his heart, up to the very hilt. That is my oath.'

Her passion terrified him. He could find nothing to say.

'I have always feared the shedding of blood,' she continued less fiercely. 'Feuds rise from the pride and ambition of men and all over the regions of the earth women must grieve over the lifeless bodies of their children. Sometimes an attempt is made to prevent the flow of blood and a woman weeps as her daughter is given in a marriage where the bonds are not affection but suspicion and hate. That is Freawaru's destiny; and on the day that the Heathobards march out to avenge the death of their former king, her beauty and diplomacy will not delay them, and she will know that the battle will bring the death of the king, her father, or of Ingeld, her lord. So I fear blood feuds, tribe against tribe. And kin against kin is worse. Yet,' and her voice was resonant again, 'yet I would not hesitate to let the blood of Hrothulf, my husband's nephew, if you were in danger. I should not consider the outcome or pay heed to future tears. Desire for power and the wickedness that is in them pushes men to the feud, but when a woman takes up the knife, she slits without scruple for the child that her body bore.'

Her resolution filled him with wonder, but he could not accept it. For it claimed him and he considered himself no longer a child whom she must protect. So, this time, he was able to say, 'There will never be need for you to spill blood on my behalf, Mother. That, if it is necessary, I shall do for myself.'

Her face changed. The taut angles were softened by

timorous hope. 'But you cannot do it yet, my son, and until that time comes we must be cautious and consider carefully all we do. Today there is a precise danger. That is why I sent for you. Hrothulf suspects Beowulf. He believes that his journey here to fight the monster was an excuse to enter our kingdom, to assess its weakness and ingratiate himself with our king. Hygelac of the Geats is powerful, huge as Beowulf in body, and the commander without question of his host and court. Neither he nor his people would ever permit Beowulf, his nephew, to succeed in preference to his sons. So Hrothulf argues that the Geat warrior seeks your father's throne. Yes,' she continued through Hrethric's interruption, 'we know he does not, but Hrothulf, desiring it himself, cannot imagine such a man wanting less and he sees everything as a threat. He and his fellow Unferth failed to discredit the warrior last night before the court and by ensuring that he met the monster alone they did not bring about Beowulf's death but contributed to his lasting fame. Now the king greets him as a son.'

'Is that not wise of him, Mother? As my cousin said, will not Beowulf strengthen my father's arm?'

She sighed. 'You speak like a simpleton, Hrethric. Your father's gratitude outruns his wisdom. He seems unaware of how men will interpret his gesture.' The prince remembered Angenga's foreboding. 'For Hrothulf, it favours a man whom he already sees as a competitor. You, he can disregard, but not the Geat. Hrothulf imagines that Beowulf will return to claim the throne on Hrothgar's death. He is determined to prevent that.'

'What does that mean?'

'There are many ways of killing a man.'

'But not Beowulf!' He could not believe it.

'His retinue is small; it scarcely filled one ship. There would be many more if Beowulf came as a king. So Hrothulf calculates that he must strike now. It might not be so difficult. Enticed on some pretext to march into the fastness, they could be overcome by followers of Hrothulf and Unferth who could be gathered into a party at least four times the number of the Geats and could be relied upon to hold their tongues.'

'But the reason, Mother! Hrothgar would want a reason and so would the Geat king.'

'The marshes are perilous to those who do not know the tracks, and who more plausible than Unferth to recount the sad story?'

'I will warn Beowulf.' His hand was already pushing the door.

'And admit to the Geat that your kinsman is treacherous? Not yet, Hrethric, though it may become necessary. Also I doubt whether warning would be enough. Hrothulf is ruthless and determined. He would set fire to Heorot and enjoy the screams of the Geats as they pummelled the barred doors if he could keep his guilt hidden.'

'Cannot you set the guards to protect him?'

'I can do nothing against Hrothulf openly, otherwise I should lose my influence over him which I have maintained for twelve years and must not risk now.'

'Beowulf shall not be sacrificed, Mother. I will speak to him myself.'

'No!' Her hands restrained him and, though she held herself like a queen, her look told him that she was imploring her future king. 'That way, bloodshed is certain. Let us try to prevent that for as long as we can. Give me time. I will find some other way. Beowulf is safe until after tonight's feast.'

He hesitated and she continued, 'I promise that I will send you a message if I have no plan. Then you may warn him. Meanwhile, I beg you not to question or interfere with anything I do. Watch and listen and behave as a brother to Beowulf tonight.'

'Very well. I will delay a little, but I do not like to leave the task to you.'

'You will please send Aeschere to me.'

'Of course.' Her face was blanched; her fingers were pressed upon the trestle for support. 'I will send him to you, who are my father's queen,' and for the first time in his life, like one of the duguth, he stretched for a hand and raised it to his lips.

His father's queen. Not until he was out of her chamber did he recall that neither of them had suggested they consult his father, their king.

The geogoth were returning, cantering across the knoll, their faces red with brine and wind and the flanks of their horses glossy with sweat. They were noisy like children as they shouted and boasted, good-humouredly mimicked one another and showed off their horsemanship before retainers who paused and grinned. They waved to Hrethric and beckoned him to join them but he shook his head.

The sun was past its height now and though the open space below Heorot was clear and unshadowed, the paths between the apartments were more wintery and dim. Making for Aeschere's chamber, Hrethric passed two men cowled by overhanging thatch. They held goblets and leant together with the ease that wine brings and Unferth's hand lay on his companion's shoulder. He was the Geat who had witnessed the monster devour Hondscio and who blamed the Scyldings for his death. Seeing these two together, linked in such strange amity, Hrethric felt his new courage seep away. He nodded but did not stop when Unferth greeted him, telling himself that the Geat, though disaffected, would remain faithful to his leader; but he knew Unferth had corrupted better men. Alarmed, he turned aside and hurried to the apartment reserved for guests. For many years it had stood empty. Now, hospitable again with fire and furs, it should not shame the Scyldings with a floor wet with blood.

But it was already guarded. Sitting with her back against the closed door, her gown folded to her knees so that her legs could warm and brown in the winter sun, was Freawaru. She smiled at his approach. Her posture was tranquil; her hands were nestled together in her lap.

'Freawaru! What are you doing here?' he asked unnecessarily.

'You can see what I am doing,' defending herself before her older brother since she imagined he would reproach her.

'Is it not time you prepare yourself for the banquet?'

'I shall go when the Geat wakes. I promised him that I would let no one disturb him.' Her eyes shone at his trust.

It occurred to Hrethric that the warrior could have no better sentinel, for although Freawaru kept intruders away, Hrothulf would know that she had not been placed there by the queen. He would assume that Wealhtheow was not attempting to thwart him.

'Beowulf is fortunate to find you, so patient and reliable, to watch over his sleep.'

'It is not a duty. I wish to do it. He will soon be gone. What else am I permitted to do for him?'

'Last night you attempted more than any of us, Freawaru. I am thankful that we found you. The monster might have

95

sought you out, if he had smelt your flesh.'

'That wasn't necessary,' she dismissed her behaviour. 'I did Beowulf a wrong in imagining that the demon could overcome him. He is greater than any monster, or any man I shall ever meet.'

Her fidelity was painful to Hrethric for it could not alter her future. He looked away and saw retainers sweeping the wide avenue and scattering sand over Grendel's last tracks. It was many years since he and Freawaru had played under those trees, before the day they had discovered the splayed prints, before the name of Ingeld had been whispered into their ears. Grendel had been defeated; their minds were no longer haunted by the dread of his claws, but other dangers remained, and his sister – promised to Ingeld, sitting at the door of her loved Geat whose life was threatened – Freawaru might be forced to suffer further terrors and distress. He wished that he could save her.

Something itched at his belt. He dropped a hand to it and felt the scramasax against his palm. Abruptly, he drew it out.

'For you, Sister,' he said, placing the dagger in her hands.

'But Hrethric! Your scramasax! Why is this?' She was surprised and charmed.

'I want you to have it. It is a day for bestowing gifts. It is not undeserved,' he mumbled. It was impossible to express his real reason.

'Then I accept it,' smiling her thanks. 'I will make a leather sheath for it and line it with strips of a new fleece, to keep your scramasax from rust.'

'It is for use, Freawaru, if ever the need comes.'

'Of course! Aren't I too old to be given toys?' But she was laughing at his seriousness and, faced with her pleasure, Hrethric could say no more.

Retainers were unknotting the Scylding banners and carrying them into the hall; wine-bearers, bent under the weight of flagons, lumbered through the doors; churls were rolling and dragging logs towards the great hearth. Some counsellors, dressed in ceremonial mantles, were strolling in the direction of the king's chamber. The banquet was imminent. Gusting over the knoll, the scent of roasting meat reminded Hrethric that he had not eaten anything since milk and a rye cake at dawn, but he no longer anticipated the feast with pleasure. He must be on his guard. Whatever happened, he must be at the Geat's side.

Meanwhile, his first duty was to deliver Wealhtheow's message, but Aeschere was absent from his chamber and the war saddle of Hrothgar had gone from the circle of gifts. The old man was carrying out his intention to select the best stallion and place the saddle upon it himself. Irritated by the delay, Hrethric started towards the stables but was halted by Stuff.

'I have put a fresh mantle and tunic in your apartment, my lord. It is time you got ready,' the man said.

'I must find Aeschere first. The queen wishes to speak with him.'

'I will attend to that.'

'It is important, Stuff. The message must not be forgotten.'

'I may be old, my lord, but my memory has not quite left me. I am unlikely to forget a message from the queen.'

Soothing his tetchy dignity, Hrethric answered, 'I was not questioning your capabilities, Stuff. It is that I am a little anxious, because I should deliver the message myself.'

The other bowed stiffly.

'You say you have put out fresh clothes? Good. I think I will also wear the corslet.' He remembered Unferth's sneers the previous day. 'It does not matter whether or not it is customary. It will be my way of honouring our guests.'

'It may be a wise decision.'

Hrethric looked at him quickly. What had Stuff heard? The man stared back, his face impassive.

'Why do you say that, Stuff? Are you suggesting that I may need it?'

The old man took his arm and turned him slowly until he faced up the knoll. Above them Heorot lazed under the waning sun. Its thatch was spun silk in the gentle light; its long wall, along which visiting thanes had ranged their shields, was girdled with the overlapping discs studded with glinting bosses. At the roof's summit, the branched gables were fringed with the pink of the evening cloud.

'Look!' Stuff pointed. 'You see he remains.'

Balanced on one tip of Heorot's carved antlers, the raven was black and solid against the sky.

'Perhaps he has eaten as much as his belly will hold and dare not trust his wings to take him home. I envy him. I hope that soon I shall feel as fat as he.'

Stuff did not loosen his grip. 'He remains. He waits for fresh carrion.'

Hrethric's breath stopped. He saw his mother's horse tethered among the ragged flowers in her garden; he saw a groom holding his father's stallion and knew that according to ceremonial custom king and queen would ride together round the knoll and down the avenue of trees; he saw thanes and counsellors with their ladies, duguth with their retainers, and all the crowding geogoth who had collected upon the grass whose colour was deepening in the fading light; and he saw that Freawaru had left her post and that the door of Beowulf's chamber was open; and he saw a huge body lying upon bloodstained furs, laced with slashes of many swords, and the raven hopping upon it, pecking into the red wounds.

The sight was too painful. It had to be dismissed. Desperate, conquering the fear with argument, he answered, 'Or perhaps the bird has smelt the feast. He claims his share. You talk like a field churl who imagines a sign in every howl of a wolf or flap of a raven's wing.'

'Yes, my prince, and I see one now. Field churls should not be despised. My father was one, and his father before him. That gives me a memory longer than my own.' He permitted a sardonic smile. 'So, as if they had happened during my own life, I possess memories of things long past and all the signs that warned men of their approach. The raven waits. His tongue does not quiver at the scent of roasting meat but at the smell of wickedness that may leave him richer flesh than scraps of sheep or pig. Field churls know the value of signs you scorn; they know the truth of sights they have seen; they can interpret the tracks of men and beast, but their wisdom is ignored by elegant lords who think themselves safe in their hall. The raven waits, though he has gorged himself on the monster's arm. And I tell you that that arm is more than a bait for the pebbles of mocking thanes.'

Then he was gone, hurrying towards Aeschere who was riding out of the stables, leaving Hrethric to gaze after him, fearful, apprehensive, trying to comprehend what the old servant meant.

# NINE

'I must sit by the king's table,' the scop said to Hrethric as they met at the doors of the hall. He plucked a string of the lyre he carried and smiled at the twanging note. 'I shall be asked to recite my lays. I am conscious of the honour and, do you know, Hrethric, I feel strangely nervous.'

'There is no need, Angenga. I am sure your skill will delight us.' He answered negligently, his attention given to the thanes and duguth filing into their places. One of Unferth's men was leading the Geat warriors to a table below the high seat but the one who nursed a piece of Hondscio's tunic next to his dagger was escorted to the table of his new friend.

'It is clear that I shall receive little sympathy from you. Young men decked out in battle armour cannot give their minds to artists' problems, particularly before a banquet,' he joked, amused by Hrethric's preoccupation. Assuming an extravagant posture, a fist pressed against his puckered forehead, he announced, 'I will find my colleague. At least he will understand the feelings of a visiting scop.'

Still watching the men taking their positions at the benches, Hrethric said, 'We have not a scop. He was one of the first to be taken. No one replaced him. When Heorot was empty at night there was no feasting. We had no need for songs.'

The scop's fist dropped to his side. 'No need for songs?' he repeated. 'No *need*? Songs are not ornaments like these swaying banners; they are not embroidery for a banquet like those scenes stitched upon the tapestries decorating these walls. Songs are the speech men cannot utter. Songs increase their pleasures and discover meaning and consolation in their pain. These last years of the Scyldings were darker than I imagined, Hrethric.'

'I did not mean to offend you, Angenga. I was thinking of other things. Do not conclude that I undervalue your craft. It was never wholly forgotten. Sometimes on a grief-swept morning my father would sing a lay.'

'Ah.' The scop nodded as if an intuition were confirmed. 'Then I am twice honoured, and have added reason not to disappoint my patron.'

'Even more may be demanded of you,' Hrethric said quietly. 'You carry your scramasax, Angenga?'

'I always bring my scramasax to a feast. How else could I enjoy the good meat?' He answered in a light tone as a retainer passed with a steaming dish, but his eyes were enquiring.

'It may be necessary to use it for another purpose. Watch carefully, Angenga. If my mother by gesture or secret word gives me a signal, we may need your sharp point.'

'So . . . perhaps the nervousness I feel is not caused by the prospect of singing in Heorot! But while I am a guest in this court, my life is at the service of your mother and the king.' Thus the scop stated the traditional obligation without pausing to ask questions, bowed, and moved towards his place.

Taking his own, Hrethric realized that the chatter was decreasing. In the curious way that a vast company will sense the approach of an expected guest, counsellors and their ladies, duguth and the nudging geogoth, the churls

101

and retainers, all broke off their talk and turned welcoming faces towards the great doors.

And this night he entered their hero, Beowulf the conqueror of Grendel, Beowulf the victor, walking at a slow pace to acknowledge their cheers. Poised as before, proud as before, he was still superior, but now he smiled and was a little jaunty as if his muscles were loosened by success. He had proved himself. It was no longer necessary for him to convince them by challenging words. Without diffidence or pretence at modesty he received their acclaim as due recognition of his service, and warrior and company were united in open joy at his feat. Not until he had reached the appointed table and retainers with trumpets had stepped into the central aisle did the cheering cease but, as Hrethric gestured Beowulf to his place, he saw that Unferth was watching them and that no shouts had passed the counsellor's lips.

A noise at his side distracted him as he welcomed the Geat. Led by a thane, a boy was slithering along the bench.

'The king has sent him, Prince,' the man said. 'Knowing that you were to sit next to the warrior, he has said that he would not have this one forgotten. He is to sit at the warrior's left hand.'

Lolling slightly within the thick collar of his mantle, the boy's face shone with scrubbing. He looked up and down the assembly with awkward jabs of his shoulders, then giggled and hid his flushed cheeks against Hrethric's arm. Thin fingers bent skew came up and hooked through his corslet's rings.

'He is my brother, Hrothmund. He will not trouble us. He was born on the first night of the demon,' Hrethric explained.

'The king desires us to remember Grendel's first visit as we celebrate his last. So I have two princes to entertain me.' But the Geat's courtesy was forced and, as Hrethric disentangled Hrothmund's fingers and lifted him on to his seat, Beowulf could not prevent a grimace of disgust.

Hrethric blushed with shame and the notes of trumpets heralding the king were strident on his ears. The sounds continued as Hrothgar, followed by the queen, Hrothulf and Aeschere, paced down the long aisle, sounds that had proclaimed the king's victories, sounds whose triumphant energy seemed to Hrethric a bitter contrast to the slobbering cripple born during Grendel's malignant dark. His frailty disgraced the manhood and reputation of the Scylding line. Hrethric wished Beowulf were not witnessing it.

Until the king paused at their table, received Beowulf formally and, turning to the young man, quietly entrusted the boy to his care.

'I shall do all that is necessary. Since he is here.'

For a moment the king's eyes widened. 'To do all that is necessary is to do less than you could,' Hrothgar rebuked. 'Do not blame him for his infirmity. It is undeserved and he cannot conquer it. We are fortunate, Hrethric, that our weaknesses are more secret and that we can overcome them if we choose.'

Then he was gone, leaving Hrethric with his face burning with resentment at the reprimand, his eyes stinging with tears of anger. Through which he saw his father standing at his high seat, holding out the precious gifts; saw Beowulf rise to receive them; saw the plaited manes and polished hooves of the eight stallions high stepping beside their grooms, and gazed at the glittering gems in the pommel of the king's saddle. To his ringing ears came the praises of the king's generosity, Beowulf's short thanks and the loud applause. Then, through Hrothgar's words of gratitude, through the assembly's hum of pleasure as their king rewarded the Geat troop also with armour and priceless gifts, Hrethric heard other sounds as his brother, excited by the cheers and the novelty of the scene, whimpered for the undemanding safety of his nurse and chamber. Not wishing the boy's blubbering to attract attention, Hrethric leaned across the Geat's empty seat.

'Be quiet!' he commanded.

The sobs were arrested, but the face that was raised to his was greased with mucus and tears. With a rough movement Hrethric scraped his hand down his brother's cheeks and cleaned it upon his sleeve. Hrothmund's mouth opened crookedly and his eyes blinked, expressing affection and trust.

Drawing back, Hrethric watched the horses returning down the aisle, led back to the stalls where they would remain until Beowulf embarked for his own land; then he examined the treasure which retainers had placed on this, the table of the honoured guest, and stretched out to adjust the position of the banner, the sword, the corslet and high helmet on their bed of white fur; while all the time he was trying to subdue the loud beating which his heart had begun at the sight of Hrothmund's face. He was not angry now.

One last gift remained and, knowing what it was, all the men and women present within the repaired and silk-decked walls of Heorot rose to their feet and bowed their heads. In the mourning silence Hrothgar lifted up a silver dish piled with bracelets and gold rings.

'Beowulf, there is one of your brave companions who cannot enjoy our feast. He died for me and my people and his name will always be honoured among us. Hondscio himself cannot receive his share of gifts as you and your company have done, so I place it in your hands as compensation for his death to his king and kin.'

'I thank you, my lord. It will be surrendered to my king, Hygelac of the Geats, for him to divide according to the dead man's worth to him and to his kinsmen's needs. This I shall do, just as I shall lay your precious treasure at his feet as customary tribute to my king.'

'I trust that Hygelac will find nothing wanting in the Scyldings' treasure,' Hrothgar answered. 'And now let us drink and eat and may this fair hall, my Heorot, be once again gilded with our pleasure and jewelled with songs.'

Immediately there was a great din. Down the two rows of tables either side of the wide aisle, men raised their goblets, toasted one another, commented upon their king's gifts, joked with friends from the outlying farms, settled on to their seats and hacked portions of meat from the dishes swiftly placed before them: pigs' crackling chines, saddles of crisp lamb, the delicate flesh of wildfowl which fell apart at their touch.

Returning to his table, Beowulf pushed the king's final gift to the edge of the white fur. It was as if he wished it out of his sight.

'My father has given just payment for the sacrifice of a warrior,' Hrethric said. He waited until a winebearer had filled their goblets. 'Shall we remember a brave man?' and raised his cup to his lips.

'I obey a prince, the son of my host,' the Geat answered and obliged with a quick sip.

Startled by his lax response, the young man was silent while retainers carved meat which Beowulf had chosen and brought sauces, tepid curds and warm speckled cakes of rye. On the left of Beowulf a thane stripped Hrothmund's meat of its skin and cut it into manageable chunks, for the boy could not handle a dagger and would soon be dabbling his hands in the mess. No longer ashamed of his brother but wishing to protect him from scorn, Hrethric tried to turn the warrior's eyes away.

'Hondscio died as many of my father's duguth and younger men also have died. There was nothing dishonourable in his death.'

'It was a disgrace to my company and the reputation of the Geat people,' Beowulf retorted. 'I do not wish to be reminded of it.'

Hrothmund was snivelling with enjoyment. Ribbons of saliva coloured brown by the juices of the meat hung from his mouth and dragged over his dish. So Hrethric continued, 'He died in your service. He could not prevent the manner of his death.'

'You have your father's kindness, Prince, but warriors must be of sterner mould and death itself cannot excuse where there is blame.'

'The demon was too strong for any man until you held him. We find no blame in Hondscio for that.'

'He had drunk too much wine,' Beowulf answered shortly. 'No Geat who undertakes a mission with me should surrender to weakness of the flesh.'

'That was a Scylding's doing, and I wish with all my heart that it was not so.'

Hrethric glanced towards Hrothulf. He was smiling as Freawaru filled his cup. Wealhtheow was laughing with the scop who sat below her. On her right, his father was reciting to Aeschere, slapping the table to the rhythm of the lines.

All down the hall men drank and feasted, reminisced about battles, showed off tricks with daggers, teased dogs to beg for succulent morsels or sent them chasing after discarded bones. It seemed impossible that treachery could lurk in such company. Yet Unferth's arm was round the shoulder of the Geat who had accused Hrethric and the man's expression had been sullen as he watched Beowulf receive the king's final gift.

'It is possible that your troop do not share your feelings. They might say that Hondscio would not have died if you had not brought them here,' the young man tried.

'Those are strange musings, Prince, more suitable for a dreamer than for men whose lives are dedicated to the sword. We do not accuse our leader if we fall under his banner,' the man answered conclusively.

The other tried again. His mother had given him no sign, yet he could se that the tables either side of Unferth were filled with Hrothulf's men. 'When a man sits in the court of another tribe and is honoured by its king, there may be dangers he did not think of as he offered himself against their common foe.'

Beowulf paused in his eating. He turned to look at Hrethric and his eyes were shrewd. 'You are honest, Prince, and brave to say so much. But there is no need to risk your own safety. My eyes and ears serve me well. Do not fear for me.'

Such assurance was not enough but the younger man could say no more. He broke a rye cake into pieces and handed it to his brother, no longer caring if the Geat saw the crooked fingers scrabbling for the crumbs.

The assembly had grown quiet. Dogs stretched at their owners' feet; men and women looked attentively towards the high seat. There was a ripple of notes from a lyre and, accompanied by the scop, Hrothgar began to recite. His voice was light and delicate but used with skill. It carried to the end of the hall, lilted among the rafters or descended to the boards at his audience's feet as it rejoiced in the battle songs of youth or sighed with the melancholy dirges of age.

'Now I will sing a lay for our chief guest. By it I pay my respects to his king for it concerns Hygelac's father and Beowulf's great uncle, Hrethel, King of the Geats. His first-born son was killed during hunting by an arrow from his brother's bow and Hrethel's grief was without remedy. He could not repay the death of one son by demanding the life of another.'

Softly the king intoned his song, emphasizing the linked words, and again their beat was stressed by a chord on Angenga's lyre.

*The hunt was halted, horns were voiceless*
*When by stag's side in heather Herebeald lay,*
*A dear-one destroyed by barb of brother.*
*And Hrethel's heart then no comfort found.*

*In the fierce grief-grasp the Geat king sorrowed,*
*No deed can avenge that arrow's death doom.*
*King for son killed cries out for vengeance,*
*But before the son-slayer sheathed is his blade.*

*Thus are mourning and misery Hrethel's companions.*
*Woe whitens his brow, withers his soul.*
*Sun shines not for him, seasons are joyless.*
*Chill is the chamber of man-child bereft.*

*So in fit of dreams father    for first-born stretches,*
*Feels no son by his side,    a space unfilled.*
*Until father forsaken,    feeding only on sorrows,*
*Fades from his soul-lock    and follows his son.*

He finished, his head bowed, his arms resting on the table. No one spoke. Then gradually another voice ruffled the stillness; at first it was shy, as if apologizing for its intrusion. It breathed upon the cadence of a word, paused, substituted another, repeated a sound, beat a rhythm to strummed notes. Until words became ordered, the voice grew stronger, and discreetly adapting his tone to Hrothgar's tender modulations, the scop improvised a sequel to the king's sad lay.

Nods and murmurs showed appreciation of Angenga's talent.

'You followed well, Scop. It is a pleasure to share my board with such a poet,' Hrothgar complimented.

'I owe my inspiration to a king.'

'Your audience is enchanted,' Wealhtheow said. 'Will you allow us more, Angenga? But perhaps, this time, a poem which dwells less upon those who sin against their own blood and the plight of their kin.' She glanced at Hrothulf's scowling face and at Unferth stirring below them.

The scop bowed. 'Then, my lady, I will sing a song about a battle that happened many winters ago, in a country beyond these shores.'

'What region do you speak of?' Aeschere asked.

'From these islands you must sail to Angelm, then follow the coast and round the northern tip where the race of Jutes once lived. There to the west, over a tumbling sea, is a land men call the new Angelm, for many of the tribe of

Angles once journeyed there and built their halls in that new land.'

'I have heard of that country,' Hrothgar mused. 'Merchants tell of its beauty.'

'That is beyond dispute. It is a fair land and turns many faces to the sea. Sometimes it rebuffs the waves with cliffs whose white dazzles the blue sky, or with towering granite at whose base the sea boils; sometimes its green turf curves to the shore where the sand sparkles like crystal or is patterned into scallops by the sucking tide; sometimes it takes the sea on its breast, its earth is soaked by the waves' salt and a traveller must learn the creeks which wind through the reeds to the land's heart. There it is veined with wide rivers, traced with valleys furred with rich grass, shaded by hills and canopied by forests so deep that a day's riding is not enough to traverse them.' He stopped, suddenly conscious of his eloquence and, flushing slightly, added, 'I try your patience. It is my own country and I shall not ever see it again.'

'No, Angenga, we breathe to your words,' Hrothgar said. Then, looking at him curiously, 'But I am surprised by your claim, for you bear yourself like a man grown among a tribe of the islands, or of the regions bordering our sea.'

'My father was a lord among the Angles and followed his prince into the new land. There I was born.'

'But do you not consider Angelm, on the lee of my fishermen's sail, the old Angelm, to be the true home of your people?'

'It was the home of my father but it is not mine. Exiled from the new Anglia, I have visited it. I have sheltered under its thin birches; I have travelled its low plains and trod the narrow paths through its bog, but the feel of its earth did not comfort me and few of its people remain. They left many winters ago, thanes and retainers, women, children and cattle, following their victorious lords, making their home in the new country where crops flourish and whose tribes could not withstand the Angles' brave hosts.'

'So, Scop, you tell us of a host which invaded the land of other tribes.' Unferth's voice disturbed the assembly. 'They defeated men who had given them no cause for enmity. Do you ask us to admire conquerors of tribes who wished to live in peace?' The counsellor frowned round at his companions. Hondscio's friend looked confused, but the rest understood that Unferth was making a comparison with the Geats.

'Come, what tribe has not warred upon another, or sought by battle to extend the boundaries of its king's power? Did not you march behind me when I conquered the tribes of these islands?' Hrothgar reasoned.

'You conquered them in order to place them under your suzerainty and protection, my king, not in order to settle among them in preference to your own good land,' Hrothulf came in smoothly.

'My people took what was theirs,' the scop answered back. Only the lift of his chin suggested that he was angered by Unferth's accusation. 'Once the new Anglia was governed by soldiers of Rome who built halls of stone to defend its shores. When they were recalled, the chiefs were left to rule the land themselves and some employed mercenaries among the Saxons to help them. But those chiefs failed in their obligation as lords; they neglected to reward the warriors for their service; they were niggardly with gifts. Such meanness was justly answered. It was repaid with battles, and the Saxon fighters and those Angles that were with

111

them won land, claiming it for the lords of their tribes. Soon these joined them, together with many who lived along the Frisian coasts.'

'A common justification for conquest! Do we understand, then, that the battle song you promised us is to glorify alien warriors who betrayed the trust of the king they served and, perverted by ambition, slaughtered his host, ravaged his land, and set themselves to rule in his place? It should be an exciting narrative – and also instructive.'

Unferth's tone was suave. He sat relaxed on the bench, satisfied that he had made his point. There was no need to press a reaction from his companions; they were muttering together and looking at Beowulf.

Hrethric's blood thumped with alarm. Angenga's choice of subject was foolhardy. It could inflame Hrothulf's supporters. He wished he could intervene, could call for another song, but he lacked the authority and there was no time.

For the scop was already answering. 'No, Counsellor, the matter of my song is not what you describe. I do not recount those early battles but one that occurred many winters after my people first ruled in many regions of their new land, a battle which I fought in, I who was the first of my father's children to be born in that country. In that fight my lord fell; his hall was sacked and his treasure taken. So I became a lonely wanderer without lord or land. That day brought me nothing but misery and grief, but I am a scop and must try to see it whole. I must try to see it from all sides, and I should be a mean and dishonest man if I did not sing the praises of the warrior who cut down my lord, a warrior who gathered a host out of the far mountains to which they had fled and who rode before them like an avenging deity armoured in wrath. The place where we fought was the hill of Baden. The name of their leader was Arthur.'

Rising to his feet, the scop began.

*Starless the sky,    soundless the dwellings*
*As our warriors waited,    a watch most drear.*
*Then sun came sudden,    struck the tree-tips,*
*Ringed the horsemen    high on the ridge,*
*Till at signal sounded,    swift down they galloped.*
*Earth took the hoof-hammer.    Morning was marred.*

*So on foam-flecked stallions    with flanks sweat-sheened,*
*Tribes under tribute    fronted our host.*
*One cried loudly,    in looks no coward,*
*'You murder-merchants,    who masters call yourselves*
*Are challenged to combat    by kin of the slain.*
*I, Arthur, address you,    an adversary fearful,*
*Leader of northmen    sworn to revenge.*
*Hill-got and cavern-whelped,    suckled on sorrows,*
*They thirst like wolves    for your womanish throats.*
*These gaunt grave-men    will grease their axes.*
*Death day for Angles    by Arthur is doomed.'*

*No words wasted    our warriors in answer,*
*But straight sprang to weapon-clash.    Our loved lord*
*Drew first the battle-iron,    the blood-dyed blade.*

*Now to the sword-beat    stamp the Angles,*
*Shoulder to shoulder    we strike at the savages.*
*Bravely the spears spike,    unsheathed is the scramasax,*
*War-metal clanging    spark-spangles the air.*

But wild are these woodmen    whirling on stallions.
Shrill are their shrieks    raging for slaughter.
Their cruel curses    claw at our flesh.
Like fox robbed of vixen,    vengeance is fanged.

Undaunted our warriors    drive at the centre,
Proud in the sword-play    we hack at the foe,
On hostile helmets    hone our trim blades.
Till through war's thicket    a tribesman thunders,
Arthur their leader    before our lord reins.
Grim glare his eyes,    ghastly his frown.
Speech he spurns now    but points to his dead.
And Arthur swings sudden,    cleaves with the cruel edge,
Axe hews the forehead.    Felled is my lord.
Breached is the bone.    The breath sighs out.

Now men mourn loudly,    matchless our sorrow.
Blood beards our cheeks,    blinkers our sight,
And red-dappled, the dear ones    drop by our lord.

I waking from wounds    weep for my fellows,
Friends war-wasted,    forage for wolves.
Hear the ghosts wailing    for their sacked wine-hall.
So I, Angenga the Angle,    alone must wander,
From Baden I turn    to trudge out my days,
Putting behind me    those plundered corpses,
The hearths of my homeland,    the love of my lord.

There was silence after the scop ended, then men rose and
drank to him, praising his skill.

'He was a noble leader. And did he free his people? Are
there no Angles now in the new Angelm?' Hrothgar asked.

'It was a single victory. Arthur is dead, though his tribe believe that once again he will come among them and lead them to regain their land. But our people remain. It is their country now.'

Hrethric heard no more, for taking advantage of the company's rising and the renewed movements of retainers, Hrothulf had left his seat and was standing behind him. 'I see you note closely what the versifier says,' he whispered in Beowulf's ear.

Turning in a leisurely manner, the Geat swung a leg and straddled his seat. 'His words command our attention. He is an accomplished performer and an excellent bard.'

'Would you agree that there is much to be learned from his story?'

'That is held to be one of the benefits of song but not, for me, the most important.'

'Now that may be a disadvantage. It would be a pity if you were to misinterpret the meaning of that verse.'

'I have heard scops say that each man makes his own meaning. He will understand only what his mind is ready to receive. What meaning do you give it, nephew of my father Hrothgar?' he asked easily.

Hrothulf flushed at Beowulf's deliberate claim. 'I would say that it teaches men to hesitate before they set foot in another kingdom, for the people are apt to take the matter unkindly and may meet the strangers with drawn swords.'

'Which is a natural and commendable thing to do,' Beowulf answered, refusing to be drawn. But then he could not resist adding, 'However, if you heard what the scop has just told the king, you will know that native tribes who resist cannot be sure of permanent victory.'

'Those Angles were defeated. The native prince Arthur

slew their lord. He slew the sons of men who had come to serve his country and stayed to usurp their master's rights. It is well to take heed of what became of that scop's lord, my friend.' His discretion had begun to slide away. 'Remember that you have a small troop, Geat.'

'I? Are we not talking of the battle by the hill of Baden, Scylding?'

At which, Hrothulf's brittle posture cracked. 'No. We are talking about you. You have wheedled your way into my uncle's favour—'

'Wheedling seems an odd description for the killing of Grendel,' the other interrupted.

'. . . You have accepted his foolish adoption and now conduct yourself as his son.'

Beowulf breathed deeply and his nostrils flexed, but his voice stayed controlled. 'It would be discourteous to do otherwise.'

'Courtesy is not your reason. Do not imagine that you deceive us. We know that you plan to claim far more than the rewards received for subduing the man-beast.' He was spitting out the words.

'My work here is finished. I desire no more than I have received. I do not seek to deceive you. You deceive yourself. I have nothing to hide. For which reason your accusations are like a louse on a bear's belly, of such insignificance that he does not stir to scratch it off.'

'Contempt is a poor weapon, Geat. It cuts less deeply than the blade. It is unwise to speak thus to me who sits by the side of a queen. You think that the king means the throne for you, rather than his own kin, but there are many in this court who will not be ruled by his choice. You risk much by your insults, Geat.'

116

His hand was at his belt, a thumb's width from his dagger slick in its sheath. Fearless, but remembering the other's great strength, he glanced quickly at Unferth and the waiting men.

'And you risk more, Scylding.' Anger was unbridled now. He kept his eyes on Hrothulf's face but Hrethric knew that he watched that gap between the thumb and the dagger's hilt and listened for the plunge of men behind. 'I am not concerned with the petty intrigues of your court. They are not worth the consideration of a true warrior. But while I am in this court I am subject to Hrothgar who is my host and calls me his son and it is he I serve and his wishes I follow. I submit to no threats from lesser men.'

'Lesser!' Hrothulf shrilled and his hand jumped the gap. But it never closed upon the hilt for at that moment a whimpering which had been an unregarded descant to his speech suddenly rose to a shriek. Hrothulf stepped back; the Geat tensed as Hrothmund's frenzied body, hands clawing the air, tongue protruding from a mouth issuing scream upon scream, fell between them. Glazed eyes showed him Hrothulf above him. His legs wrenched up; his twitching arms wrapped over his face as he tried to protect himself against the man whose menace jerked his body in spasms, split his throat with continuing screeches, and drenched his skin in a sweat of fear against which he had received no potion as he had against Grendel on former nights. Choking, squirming, with a great effort he arched his back, rolled from his cousin's threat and knocked against the Geat's feet. And before the stunned assembly Beowulf bent down, lifted the malformed boy, and held him against his chest.

## TEN

Immediately people were rushing forward to assist him. Freawaru and the scop reached him first. Through the babble of voices all round them, Hrethric heard Beowulf say, 'He is too heavy for you, my lady,' as Freawaru reached up.

'His sickness has returned. He cannot help it,' she answered, stroking the boy's knotted hand. 'Something must have made him afraid.'

'Yes, though there was no need.' He laid Hrothmund carefully upon a litter held by two thanes and as they carried him away, attended by Freawaru and his nurse, he added, 'But even in his terror, he prevented further blood.'

'I saw,' Angenga said quickly, for the noise around them was diminishing. 'I will stay here.'

'Your place is by the king's table, Scop; your scramasax drawn for him. I still have a prince by my side. He is alert to danger — a fellow very eager with cautions.' Beowulf spoke lightly but for a moment Hrethric's arm was squeezed in the man's grip. 'Yet I do not think they will be necessary tonight.'

They looked round them. The confusion had passed; guests were easy again in their seats and raised goblets which, at the command of Hrothgar, were being refilled by bustling retainers. Hrothulf had returned to the king's table where he was whispering to the queen. She nodded and smiled. Recovered from the shock of Hrothmund's shrieks, she sipped her wine and looked composed.

'You may be right,' the scop agreed.

Then they saw Hrothulf lean against her. His face dipped close to her ear and for an instant the goblet in her hand shook.

'Serene and golden, I am a sheaf standing high above the stubble, rewarding the labourers' toil with my beauty and abundance, but a black crow pecks at my ears. Greedy, he would fill his maw, leaving the husbandman and children empty, a prey to famine or his companions' sharp beaks,' Angenga extemporized. 'Is not that true, Hrethric, Prince of the Scyldings, descendants of the Sheaf?' and without further words, he hurried back to his seat below the queen.

She had already risen, and as she waited for silence there was nothing strange in her manner. Only by a swift glance at her son did she acknowledge the crisis and signal that a decision had been made.

'Do not question anything she does,' he whispered to Beowulf, pulling him to his seat. 'We must follow where she points.'

'Am I not her guest?' he answered impatiently. 'Also, I respect her wisdom.' Seeing that Freawaru had returned, he beckoned her to the empty place by his side and asked as the noise receded down the benches, 'The prince?'

'He sleeps.'

'I hope his sleep is as peaceful as mine was under your vigil, Princess Frea, rightly named Waru, watchful care. You are a most gentle sister,' he thanked her softly, and Freawaru smiled, her cheeks flushed.

'Our feast is almost ended. We have eaten and drunk well. We have listened to songs, for which we thank you, our king, and you, scop from the far new home of the

Angles,' Wealhtheow began. 'For the first time for twelve winters this hall has echoed with the sounds of men's pleasure while the earth was roofed with the darkness of the night. For that we thank Beowulf and his company. You, my king, have already given priceless gifts; I, too, have gifts for our chief guest, but before I ask him to receive them I have a request to make of you.'

Prepared to indulge her, though slightly puzzled, Hrothgar sat back in the high seat, while she faced the assembly, her demeanour tranquil. But when she inclined to the king as she began her request, the urgency which she wished to convey to him could not be wholly disguised from her guests. They shifted with interest. Hrothulf, his face sullen, looked at her intently and Unferth flicked warning glances at his men.

'It is not a favour to ask easily, my lord, for it suggests disapproval of your generosity but I must ask it for the sake of your people and the princes of your dynasty. It concerns your naming Beowulf as your son. That shows your love and gratitude towards the warrior but I beg you to reconsider it. Beowulf and his company have been rewarded. You have given to them freely for they deserve the most precious treasures that we have, and you, King Hrothgar, are already famous for your munificence and will never be accused of a grudging observance of cost.

'But the inheritance of your throne is a matter of state and affects your people, and it is right that one of the Scylding dynasty should follow after you. Bequeath it to one of your own blood, my lord.' She paused, and while Hrothulf smiled at the ambiguity, others in the hall glanced towards Hrethric and murmured their approval. 'It will be secure, my king. Here, in the lovely Heorot that you built, you have my oath that the Scylding dynasty will continue and its king will sit secure upon this throne.'

She had finished and for a moment her body sagged with the effort she had made. Then she was straight again and smiling as Hrothgar raised her hand to his lips. 'It shall be as you wish, my queen. I cannot refuse such understanding and beauty. I know that Beowulf also will bow to your request and that nothing will loosen the bonds of love between him and myself – between him a warrior taut with strength and myself whose muscles are now shrunk that once swung a battle sword to victory against enemy hosts.'

'My loyalty and fellowship are yours, my lord, King Hrothgar of the Scyldings.' Beowulf's voice resounded down the hall.

In the applause that followed, Hrethric saw fingers search for his mother's hand that was hidden from the king, and Hrothulf's dark head bent as his mouth sucked at her palm. Then she had dragged away and was walking towards their table while Hrothulf laughed, tossed his belt and scramasax among the litter of plates in a gesture of relaxed victory, and called for more wine.

Her words were scarcely audible as an attendant laid her gifts upon the white fur. Beowulf touched the finest, a wide collar of beaten gold set with gems. 'I shall honour this not only as a gift from a queen but in remembrance of a brave woman,' he said quietly.

On every side of them people were cheering; cheeks were round with pleasure at the sight of more gifts; wine and good food made all men companions and amorous towards the women.

'My request was necessary,' Wealhtheow said.

'That does not deny your courage.'

'You understand?'

'Yes.' Amid the noise, it was a private conversation between them.

'He believes that I shall help him take the throne. I must wait until Hrethric sits among the duguth.'

'You deceive for a good reason.'

'You believe me, Beowulf? You do not think that I deceive you?' she appealed.

'No, lady. I know that you are true.'

'I may not be strong enough. He has many followers. I may not be strong enough to prevent him. His tongue can be as persuasive as his sword.' She shuddered and rubbed at the palm that had received Hrothulf's kiss.

'There are many loyal ones that will support you.'

'They are old, like Aeschere. They are too weak to defend even themselves. He laughs and calls them grey heads. I fear for my sons. Beowulf, will you watch over them? Will you come to their defence if they need you? Will you be a brother to them as the king would wish?'

'One of your princes has watched by my side this night. The other threw his body between me and his cousin's dagger. I have learnt that Freawaru attempted a more terrible sacrifice. You ask for nothing that I do not already owe.'

He looked round them. The assembly was rising. Hrothgar was standing by the high seat, waiting for the queen to join him before leading his guests from the hall. Hrothulf, his arm round his friend's shoulder, was joking with his men. Already retainers were beginning to clear the tables and move benches to the walls.

'I will do what you ask, my lady.' Before Hrothulf he had

scorned the intrigues of their court. Now he said, 'My sword would not remain in its scabbard if another claimed the throne. Should your children be in danger, I will come to their aid. I and my Geats.' He bent to the great collar Wealhtheow had given him and, lifting it to his lips, sealed his promise with a kiss.

Relief drew the colour back to her cheeks. 'I thank you, Beowulf', was all she could say, then she had returned to her husband and, followed by the chief counsellors, they left the hall.

'Your apartment is ready, and the quarters of your company, my lord Beowulf,' Aeschere said by their side. 'The queen has ordered a guard. It will be discreet. I have seen to that.'

So that was why she had summoned the old man, Hrethric thought. Wealhtheow had anticipated all that might happen and was ensuring that Beowulf was protected. It did not surprise him that Aeschere was in her confidence.

'Thank you, Counsellor. It is a considerate precaution. Otherwise, I should not have allowed myself to sleep.'

'Yes; so we thought, but that is unnecessary now and I trust that your rest will be quiet.'

'And yours, Aeschere. You will welcome the peace of your chamber after your work today.'

'Where there is pleasure there is no task, my lord; and tonight I shall sleep in Heorot. Until the coming of the monster it was the custom of the duguth to remain and now, because of you, they can revive that practice. Look, they are preparing to sleep.'

The tables had been pushed back. Two thanes were filling the hearth with fresh logs and retainers were laying down bolsters and furs within the arc warmed by the fire and stippled by the tawny light of its flames.

'I have a strange whim to stay with them,' Aeschere continued. 'To celebrate our release. Though I confess that my old bones would be more comfortable on my own bed. But I wish to spend one last night in my lord's hall.'

'Surely there are many nights left to you, Aeschere.'

'No, my lord. I have reached an age when each night could be my last.'

'This is melancholy talk.'

'It may seem so to you, but age has a joy which youth does not know. Young men open their eyes to the day's light without surprise or rapture, but an old man who has waited for death in the darkness greets each new morning as a hallowed gift.'

They watched as, shuffling a little with tiredness, he made for the bolster which his servant had laid on one side of the hearth, apart from the rest, and saw him wince as the man lifted off the ceremonial mantle.

'He still feels the wound he received in battle, saving my father from an enemy sword,' Hrethric explained. 'He was once a brave warrior.'

'There is bravery among the Scyldings.' Then, as if embarrassed by the admission, Beowulf said good night abruptly and followed the thane who waited to accompany him to his bed.

Freawaru had left with the queen. The scop, too, had gone. Beowulf and his troop were striding away. Guests were lodged in the apartments of friends. Many of the retainers had returned to their huts; the rest were propped against bolsters at the end of the hall. At the hearth, the members of the duguth were stretched on their furs and the light from the burning wood polished faces that were closing in sleep. Among them, Hrethric saw many of Unferth's men. Breathing quietly or snoring hugely, they slept as their companions. Either they had received no order to attack the Geats or the effects of wine prevented them. Their sprawled bodies disturbed the hall with no hint of menace and Beowulf slept in his chamber guarded by thanes loyal to the queen. Hrethric could suspend vigilance until the morning.

Heorot was at peace. It was no longer a place of slaughter, a hall shunned at night, bare of all ornament, furnished with nothing except benches and trestles mottled with dark stains. It was the Heorot his father had conceived and was now as it had been in former days. It was the place where men slept without fear. Its walls had enclosed their feasting; its roof had returned the cadences of their song. And though huge and imposing it could be as intimate and welcoming as a private chamber, accepting, without loss of dignity or grandeur, the bones and crumbs littered over the floor, the mongrels supine under the trestles, the wheezing of men lying in random postures round the earth. Hrethric could see the shape of banners hanging in the rafters and, on the border of the firelight, the armour of the sleeping men which was flattened by shadow or sprang into burnished form as the flames shrank down or swelled. For each man a corslet hung on the wall; a helmet and sword lay on the bench below. It was the first time Hrethric had seen the hall like this and for the first time he thought he understood why it held such a place in his father's heart.

He moved towards a bolster by Aeschere but was stopped by a whisper which came from the shadowed benches behind him.

'Why, Stuff! Is it you? Why are you here?'

125

'I have waited to walk with you to your chamber, my prince.'

'I am staying here, Stuff.'

'But it is time you returned, my lord. I have built a fire there. The night is cold.' He was blundering through the trestles, clumsy in his haste.

'There is a fire here. You coddle me, Stuff, as if I were a girl.'

'No, my lord.' Reaching him, the man hooked a hand over Hrethric's arm. 'I serve a young man who is my king's son. Shall I be accused that I neglected his trust?'

'Of course not. It is ridiculous to exaggerate such an unimportant matter.'

'It is not unimportant. I beg you to come with me. Quickly. There are few hours left before dawn.' He glanced over his shoulder to the unlit threshold of the hall.

'The demon is dead,' Hrethric exclaimed impatiently. 'Your famous memory has been drowned in too much wine.'

'I have drunk nothing tonight. That would have been folly. For there is other danger, and I kept watch.'

'I believe that is over for the time and there is a guard on Beowulf's chamber.' No pretence was necessary before Stuff.

'I am not concerned about the Geat. My duty is to you. Please, my lord, come. You will be safe in your chamber.' His speech was sharp and urgent and he was pulling on Hrethric's arm.

'You are crazed, old man. What is it you are afraid of?'

'I have already told you, Prince. It is your memory that is drowned. The monster's arm still swings above those doors and the bird roosts in the open wound.'

'What of that? Your country tales are tedious, Stuff.'

The warmth from the hearth was seductive. He wanted nothing more than to lie down and sleep. Unable to tolerate Stuff's pleading further, he pulled his arm out of the man's grip; and saw the despair in his eyes and the hand beckoning to the shadows.

'You have another?' he cried before the figure became distinct and he recognized the mother of Oslaf.

'Forgive me, my lord. I also come to implore you.'

Her presence astonished him but politeness demanded tolerance. He turned his back on the slumbering men and asked, 'What is it you wish to say?'

'That the signs tells of danger, my lord.'

'What are the signs?'

'The raven waits. It no longer feeds upon the arm. It waits for fresh carrion. There will be a death.'

He remembered Aeschere's words. 'A natural death?'

'No, my lord. It nestles in flesh violently ripped from the body. This death also will be violent.'

'Who brings this danger?'

'We do not know, Prince, but the hand draws it.'

'The hand? Explain it to me.'

'The hand of the monster, my lord.' She paused and for a moment she clenched her mouth tight against its trembling. She was talking of the hand that had crushed her son. 'It is not closed. The fingers curve up from the open palm. Like this.' She held out her hand in the attitude of a beggar. 'It beseeches.'

They were silent. A draught sneaked through their mantles and they shivered.

'What does it beseech?' Hrethric whispered.

'We do not know, but it is evil. Only evil can come to its call.'

127

'Land churls murmur,' Stuff supported her. 'They remember that the counsellor Unferth murdered his kinsman. They say like calls upon like. The hand is evil; it murdered many and may draw another to kill again.'

The shadows shifted and he saw again Unferth leering as he filled Hondscio's goblet; he saw his figure menacing under the eaves; he saw Hrothulf's hand sliding towards his scramasax's hilt; he saw his arm tight on Wealhtheow's shoulder and his mouth biting into her palm.

'Will the evil be from man or spirit?' he asked through dry lips.

'They say it is neither. Not a true man or a spirit which we would know,' Stuff answered.

'That is a senseless riddle. What use are signs if you cannot read them?'

'It is we, not the signs, that are at fault. The meaning will become clear. But there is one that needs no reading. The monster's claw hangs above the doors of this hall. It is to Heorot that the evil will come. Please, my lord, return to your chamber. You are our prince. Do not wilfully endanger your life.'

A log split open; a few skinny flames raced along its core, then the wood crumbled to ash. The crescent of light round the hearth was diminishing, sucking the darkness into its shrinking edge. For one instant Hrethric was persuaded.

Then the woman whispered, 'Oslaf would have desired it, my lord,' and he knew that it was impossible to do what they wished.

'You are wrong, lady. Oslaf would not have encouraged cowardice. He gave his life for his king. He was killed by that demon whose hand now brings another evil to this hall. I will wait for it here. Whatever it is, I will confront it.

To do otherwise would be a betrayal of the courage of my dead friend.' And though his limbs trembled as he spoke, he felt relief and a tired satisfaction that at last the decision was made.

His resolution silenced further appeals. 'May the deity look kindly upon you, my lord,' Stuff said and, turning, they felt their way between the trestles and benches and out through the unseen, remote doors of the hall.

Heorot was changed now. The banners above him, moving in the draught, were the giant wings of birds which hovered in wait for his flesh; the brindled dogs circled him like a pack of wolves; the bones on the floor were the gnawed ribs of slaughtered men; the last flames in the hearth were running, luminous blood. Darkness was claiming the hall, pushing back the weak firelight, making the cheeks of the men cavernous, hollow as skulls. The old terror came to him. Stumbling, he lunged over the shrouded bodies, lifted a log and dropped it into the hearth. For a moment it stifled the flames, then they curled round it and in the new light Hrethric saw Aeschere's face. It was tranquil, the wrinkles smoothed to shallow lines, the lids resting over the eyes lightly as fallen leaves. A different fear took him. He bent over and put his cheek to the worn face and did not remove it until he was sure of the shallow breaths.

'Rest well, old man,' he murmured.

Sitting beside him, regarding the counsellor's mild face, the young man was less oppressed by the lurking darkness. The hall recovered some of its former features and Stuff's predictions seemed wild. 'Country superstitions!' he declared to himself, but he did not stretch for his bolster; he remained squatting on the floor by the side of the old man.

129

There was comfort here, by Aeschere. His untroubled breaths were reassuring; fear was an incongruous emotion when Hrethric looked at the steady face and remembered it, solemn and undismayed, as Aeschere answered a challenge from Hrothulf; remembered his firm but not harsh voice as he reprimanded Hrethric as a child; remembered the arms, strong and dependable, that had carried him through the forest to the sacred glade.

Aeschere's nearness strengthened him but it could not combat his loneliness. What had the scop said? 'Speech is a comfort. It should be passed round like a wine cup among friends'; but there was no one to talk with him, keeping the fears at bay, as there had been the previous night. His forehead ached. Behind it, his mind clouded; forms round him were indistinct; his head lolled then jerked up and he peered into the greying embers on the hearth as if, by forcing his eyes to see, he would capture the thoughts that were retreating, sliding off the edge of his brain.

'Songs are the speech men cannot utter,' the scop had said before tonight's feast, and he tried to repeat the song about Arthur, kept his lips moving though he could not remember the words, kept his lips moving and his head nodding to the well-known rhythm of the lines. And round him, the breathing of his father's duguth joined the rhythm of his wordless song. It beat in his head; it followed the motion of his lips; it continued as his eyes closed; it went on after his lips were still and he listened to it as he slept. He heard it rise and fall, heard it expand, grow harsh, break into uneven pants and blow hot and rancid on his face. As points of fire dug into his neck.

He was borne up. He was thrashing in the air. He was pulled against a body. His waist was encircled by an arm.

His calves were fettered by grinding thighs. A hand was tearing at his corslet. He was straining, stretching over the thick arm for his scramasax and his fingers found nothing but an empty sheath. There was a growl against his neck as nails were snagged in his corslet's welded rings. They tugged free and came down over his throat. Then there was a sharp cry. He was thrown off. His head smacked against a bench and through the fog of pain he saw the scratch of Aeschere's sword across a naked back, saw it drop as the warrior doubled under a swinging blow, saw his inert body lifted and crushed against swarthy, pendulous breasts, and watched it carried through the mass of rising, shouting men.

His head pounding, his neck streaming blood, Hrethric staggered down the long aisle. But it was too late. Only the sound of steps and a cackle of triumph remained in the darkness. Hrethric leant against the doors of Heorot, called out, again and again, the name of the old counsellor, and wept as the vomit gushed from his throat.

## ELEVEN

'It was a woman,' Stuff reported to the scop.

'A woman?'

'I saw her shape clearly,' Hrethric said. He winced as the servant wiped his bleeding neck.

'The omens suggested that it would be no man,' Stuff muttered.

'All living things must have birth,' Angenga replied.

The other's nursing was arrested. 'You think it was the monster's dam?' and the duguth standing round them stepped back at his words.

'It could be no one else. Are there no reports of such a one?'

'Long ago a fieldman said he had seen two figures stalking through the marsh mists, but only idle crones paid him attention. He was a notorious drinker and wine doubled his vision. And for the twelve winters that the demon visited us, only he was seen.'

'His death has roused her. She has removed Grendel's arm.'

'Yes.'

'She came to avenge her son.' Angenga spoke for them all.

'It is worse than before,' Stuff murmured. His look was hopeless and his hands dabbed listlessly at Hrethric's wound. The men had moved away and were frantically gathering up their armour.

'You are badly torn,' the scop addressed Hrethric. 'But you are fortunate you were wearing your corslet. It saved you.'

'No. I was saved by Aeschere. She carried him away.' He closed his eyes, not trusting himself to describe what he had seen.

'I did not know that.'

They were silent. The duguth, fastening on their corslets, paused and bowed their heads. One stepped quietly forward and laid Aeschere's sword on the bench by his prince.

'A life for a life,' Angenga intoned.

His words were taken up by the king, walking slowly with his retinue down the long aisle.

'That is a bitter truth, Scop, but justice is a stern teacher and offers no consolation in our loss.' His eyes rested on Hrethric, on the red holes at his nape, on the jagged flesh of his throat, and he watched the queen and Freawaru bend over him to assist Stuff, but his concern was not with the living. 'His mother takes her revenge. I never counted that danger. Joy in her son's defeat pushed from my mind the possibility that one might be sorrowing over his foul corpse. A man calls upon his kin, even as his tongue thickens in his mouth. And kin answer. So she came, and her vengeance is terrible to me.'

He was leaning against a table, looking down at Aeschere's sword. 'He was the friend of my youth. He was the warrior by my side. He was the counsellor closest to my hand. His loyalty and love were infinite and there was no spot which blemished his life. I knew no man better than he. And she has taken him from me.' He looked up. His face was waxen and rigid as a mask. Nothing moved on it except tears which seeped from the staring eyes.

'He saved your son, my lord. He did not fear death,' Angenga said.

'She took Aeschere in exchange for her son,' Hrothgar continued. It was as if he had not heard the scop's words. 'She has bereft me of my dearest friend. With a woman's instinct she strikes where she knows there will be the greatest hurt. Men continue the feud but when a woman avenges her kin she fights without compassion or remorse. A woman will slit the throat of her own husband to protect the child that she bore.' Hrethric heard the echo of his mother's words.

'She has removed the support of my life. I rejoiced at the death of her son; she now rejoices over the lifeless body of my friend. She acted as she must; but I tell you that the duty of a subject to his king, a king to his subject, is stronger even than the bonds of blood. It is strange that I had imagined a different doom at the end of my days.' His glance touched his wife and children, then rested on Hrothulf, while his listeners gradually understood his intention.

'It is not for you to go, Hrothgar,' the queen cried out, voicing their consternation.

'And it is not for you, Wealhtheow, to question the decision of your king,' he answered. The tears were dry now. Pushing himself from the table, he commanded, 'Fetch me my corslet. Bring me my helmet. Take down my sword and shield from the wall. Tell the grooms to prepare my horse and go out to the village and bring back the fieldman who claims he once saw the demon's dam. He will guide me to her lair.'

Astonished, stopped by the queen's agitation, none of the duguth moved. 'Go!' Hrothgar shouted. 'Do as I bid you! He who hesitates at my command will learn what it is to trifle with his king,' and, forced to obey, the men hurried from the hall.

'I beg you, Hrothgar.' The queen was pulling at his arm. Hrethric had risen and the scop was by the king's side.

'This is a request I cannot grant you, my queen.' He lifted her hands away and unlatched the gold clasp of his mantle. 'Wine!' he called.

'She will not return. She has taken one life for her son's. She is satisfied.' Wealhtheow's voice was high.

'She must be killed. It is a breed which pollutes the beauty of my kingdom, and it is Aeschere's life she has destroyed.'

'As she will destroy yours.' Unmindful now of the listeners, she was on her knees, twisting the cloth of his mantle between her hands. Behind her, Freawaru was crying. 'You will not withstand her. It is long since you raised your sword in battle.'

His fingers had once been brown round a jewelled hilt. Now they were white and slender, but they did not tremble as he held the golden cup.

'It is painful to be reminded that one is old, Wealhtheow, but age will not hinder me from attempting to requite the death of my friend.'

'No! No! You do not owe him your death. You owe us your life. Your children, your kingdom, should be your first care.'

'I have ruled through many long winters. Others will fill my place. Some believe that they can do so better than I. But I am weary of it. I have given my vigorous manhood and weakening age to this kingdom's care. Now you must allow me to offer my death where I please.'

She shrieked. The sound clashed against the rafters and

135

one, walking up the night-hidden knoll, quickened his pace. 'It must not be!' she cried stridently and turned upon the counsellors who had accompanied the king. 'Can you not prevent it? Do you watch while your king undertakes this vengeance? It is a subject's duty to ride out for his lord. I will reward your service. I will deny you nothing on your return.'

She flung out her hands; her palms were open in appeal towards a figure standing apart. Hrothulf looked back at her frowning. He did not move forward. And even at that moment, even through the fog of pain and the cries of his mother's anguish, Hrethric realized that at last Wealhtheow had revealed her true passions and loyalties and that Hrothulf was no longer deceived.

But there was no time to consider what might result, for his mother was still imploring, 'Is there no one who will seek out the monster's dam, no one to come when I beg, no one to take upon himself the burden of my lord?'

'I will do so, Mother,' Hrethric answered, but his swollen throat muted the words and they were overlaid by others coming down the long hall.

'It shall be my task, lady.' Approaching, Beowulf stretched out and for a second he grasped her beseeching hands, then he turned to the king. 'You will permit me, my lord? You will grant me this honour of venturing in your place?'

'This is not a matter for the challenge of a Geat warrior. I go for Aeschere.'

'My lord, no member of a family is exempt from the feud and a man's children will bear the sword of their father. Hrethric has offered, but he is already wounded. So I come, not as a Geat warrior but as the son you would have me be in your heart.' At his shoulder, a flambeau flared.

'The service you came to perform is completed. I cannot allow you to risk your life again.' The warrior's mantle hung open, and Hrothgar traced his fingers over the bruises which striped the taut chest.

'I escaped unharmed. I shall try to do so again.'

Lit by torches, their expressions conveyed an understanding more exactly than their words.

Beowulf said, 'You have won your fame as a conqueror. Let me continue. Let me serve you with my younger strength.'

'That is unnecessary. She is weaker than her son. She is a woman merely.'

The Geat returned the king's smile. Then, more soberly, 'That is true: she is a woman. But she fights for her son. Therefore she is the more deadly.'

'And a son shall fight for me,' Hrothgar answered and with a small flourish, raised his goblet to his lips.

There were no cheers; only a sigh from the surrounding listeners disturbed the still air. There were no exclamations of wonder; the duguth who had carried out the king's orders spoke quietly together as they pulled on their corslets. There were no toasts; Unferth was adjusting his ringed harness and Hrothulf was sighting along the blade of his sword. There was no formal praise but Wealhtheow stroked the Geat's mantle as she passed. Instead of wine, Freawaru handed to Beowulf a bowl of frothing milk.

'I shall go at once,' he said to the king. 'Please order a thane to wake my men.'

'It is not yet day.'

'So much the better. Darkness is an advantage.'

'But makes the journey more hazardous,' Angenga pointed out.

'There is no other alternative,' Beowulf answered curtly. 'Is her lair known to any of these men?' He was in command, the professional fighter.

'A fieldman has been sent for.'

'Good. We start when he arrives.'

Turning to Hrethric, he examined the pitted neck. 'It is a hand like her son's and as large. Did she lift you thus?'

When the other had described her attack, he demanded, 'What was your size against hers?'

'Mine seemed nothing. My feet were held between her thighs.'

'Ah,' the man nodded and his eyes went over the younger one, measuring his height. 'Huge as her son, too. And how did she tear your throat?'

'She could not reach my chest through my corslet. Her nails caught in the rings.'

'So; she trusts to her claws. Like a cat. Was she clothed?' and he winced with distaste as Hrethric shook his head. 'I will not wrestle naked with a she-monster. I must wear my armour. Like yours, it may protect me against her nails. One of the duguth tells me that she was angered by Aeschere's sword. From that I do not assume that she fears weapons, but I will go fully armed. Instruct the men to collect their spears,' he said to the first of his troop who approached him, bearing his corslet and shield. 'I will tell them shortly what I intend.

'Let Freawaru bind up your wounds. Then you should rest,' he addressed the prince more gently.

'I am coming with you.'

'It will be a painful ride.'

'Not as painful as Aeschere's death.'

'And I know it will be borne with equal courage. I see

your father, too, is determined to accompany us.'

He gestured to where Hrothgar stood. He was ready for the journey. A cloak brushing his ankles protected him against the cold of the last hours of night and when the fur opened with his movements, they saw the corslet glint. Near him, a thane, himself armed, held the king's helmet and shield.

The Geat continued, 'I cannot prevent him, but I shall see that he does not meet danger. That has been promised to me. Please tell the queen I have said that.'

He left to confer with his men while Freawaru, ready with dry cloths, began to cover Hrethric's still bleeding wounds.

'Do you think he will come back?' she asked.

'I cannot say.'

'But he defeated the man-monster.' She was desperate for his reassurance.

'His evil was greedy and malicious. He killed without provocation. His reason was hidden to us and unknown to our laws. But she had cause. There was justice in her coming.'

'Beowulf fights to repay Aeschere's death. Will not the deity bless him and uphold him against the murdering dam?'

'Perhaps; but the outcome will be according to the chance of the feud.'

'How can you say that, Hrethric? Beowulf is stronger than she.'

'Perhaps.'

'He defeated the other here in the darkness.'

'Yes; and no other man could do that. Yet you must remember that, once matched, the demon was at a disadvantage for he was a visitor, uninvited to our hall. Now Beowulf must contend as the first monster did. He must invade the dam's lair where he has no right.' He wished he could find lying answers to ease her distress.

'You will help him, Hrethric? I do not wish him to die.'

'I will, if it is possible.'

'You must take the scramasax you gave me.' Offering it to him, for the first time she realized that its absence had left him unarmed. 'Hrethric! Last night, before the she-monster, you had no weapon! I had it! You could not defend yourself. These wounds are because of me.' She was appalled; her hands were at her cheeks.

'It would have been little help, Freawaru. You are not to blame. I gave it to you and you must keep it. You may need it, one day, more than I do now. I have my weapon. It has cut through many battles and a man may trust in it.'

Taking up Aeschere's sword, he joined the men assembled by the doors.

The preparations were completed. All the men wore their armour and helmets, and many were wrapped in thick cloaks which angled over the bar of the covered swords. Shields were rested on hips as the host waited.

'I expected you would carry that,' the scop commented, pointing to Aeschere's sword, and Stuff buckled a scabbard at Hrethric's waist.

Fastening the prince's long fur, the servant said, 'The queen sends you these.' They were a helmet and shield which Hrethric had never seen before.

So, without opposition, his decision to follow the duguth was accepted. Less than two days before, he had attended for the first time the king's council. This morning he was permitted to ride with his host. The honour had been conferred on him earlier than his age required, but he felt no vain jubilation.

'You are coming also, Angenga?' The scop was draped in the balding fur he had worn at their first meeting.

' "No member of a family is exempt from the feud",' he quoted Beowulf. 'Nor is any member of the household, and I am one whilst I remain your guest. Though there is little useful that I can do. I think that it is unlikely I could charm an enemy into submission with my tongue.'

The doors were opened. Men were mounting their horses. Grooms were handing up the long spears.

'May the deity guide you, my lord, and you, Scop,' Stuff said.

'If the deity intends to guide us, she has chosen a most miserable deputy,' Angenga remarked.

Cowering under Beowulf's large hand, the fieldman was pushed towards the warrior's horse. His tunic was splashed with mud; sweat moulded his coarse hair to his head. He gaped at the armed host, started at the clash of a sword, blinked at the flash of a spear or an abrupt command. Work in the fields and rest in a village hut had given him no experience of court or the accomplishments of warfare, and he was more intimidated by the proximity of the weapons and fighters than comforted by the promise of their protection. White jowled, he cringed by Beowulf's horse, yet there was a furtive slant to his face and, as he led Beowulf forward at the head of the Geat troop, his walk was uncertain. It reminded Hrethric of Stuff's reference to the man's habits. He was also disquieted to recognize that the man came from one of Unferth's farms. 'Faster!' he heard Beowulf urge. It was hard to imagine a more reluctant guide.

It was still night. A few stars diluted the darkness to a featureless grey but they relied on their horses to keep along the directed path. Down the avenue the host went, a compact squadron which lengthened to a double column as they turned into a narrower track through the wood. Behind the Geats rode the duguth led by their king; at the end came Hrethric and the scop. There was little speech: an occasional warning as they skirted a fallen branch, a sudden oath as a horse slithered down the edge of a rut. Sounds came from the creak of saddles, the clink of armour and the creatures of the wood disturbed from sleep. Roosting birds broke through dry branches. A fox barked. The twigs of a low bush twanged at a deer's startled rush. In the draught of the host's passage, dead leaves rolled scratching over the stones or crackled under the horses' hooves. As these noises lessened, they knew they were moving out of the dense heart of the wood, and when they felt the weight of the darkness lift, by an infinitesimal measure but detectable, they knew that the trees were no longer above them and that they were on the open heath.

Here there was no track to confine them, and the lines began to open out as horses stumbled over tussocks or reared as a bird rose and clapped against their chests. Anticipating the danger of men separated, Beowulf sent back an order and they travelled as before, stallions' heads blundering into haunches, and swaying flanks knocking against the adjacent rider's thighs. In the darkness the ground was far from them, covered by bunched ling which snared their horses' steps or reached at times to their bellies' height. Experience not sight told them that the sanded floor of the heath was holed by the mouths of burrows and they rode with senses tense to check the lurch of a horse, the abrupt twist into a hollow which could bring him down.

'This is a poor way to heal a new wound,' Angenga said.

'It is not painful,' Hrethric lied to the scop's unexpressed question. 'And the cloths are good against the cold.'

For the air cut into their flesh like iced steel. Out there, without shelter of trees or high bushes, they rode exposed. The sparse stars pricking the darkness gave off, not light, but cold. Their sharp points jabbed and stung. The men journeyed on, half submerged by the stiff scrub of the heath, and their backs speared by the sky's glacial thrusts.

But the cold weakened as the path descended. The air was flocked with snow. It brushed against their faces; its soft touch warmed their hands, and they laughed. Geats and Scyldings together, they laughed as the flakes starred their furs, as they pearled their shields. Like children they greeted the snow, sieved it through fingers, sucked it upon their tongues, enjoyed its hesitant beauty and its mild stroke which smoothed away the wind's hurt. The flakes drifted out of the remote sky. They covered the earth with a white down which picked out tufts and draped over shorter grasses. Released from the bonds of the heath, the horsemen trotted downwards and laughed again as they felt pliant mosses under their horses' hooves and heard the rattle of pebbles as they forded a steam.

Happy at these white flakes speckling the greyness, reassured by the firmer ground under their feet, the host chattered. Men exchanged jokes; some chanted a ribald song; all encouraged their horses like men eager for the fight. But gradually their talk diminished. For the snow lost its brilliance; colourless, its flakes splashed over them and turned to slush beneath their horses' hooves. Slithering, jostling one another, they travelled silently with heads lowered, and the wet snow fell upon their necks, ran round their jaws and dropped coldly from their chins. Not one called out as he felt his horse shift nervously under him, but a shiver swept through them all.

Reluctantly they had admitted something they had fearfully suspected. The melting snow at their feet had given to slush whose nature had altered. They had reached a new region, the region of the marsh.

The pace became slower. The columns joined and grew into a single line and each man sat tense, trusting that the one in front would not lead him off the path. Hooves sank into the spongy surface, thrashed through concealed pools, pushed against sharp reeds. The ground parted, closed and tugged at their steps. It lifted and flung up gouts of mud which slid down helmets and licked over foreheads and cheeks. Under their masters' trembling touch, the horses were restive. They snuffed and whinnied and strained to break free.

And two suddenly did so. There were neighs, shouts, orders, great splashings, the clang of armour, a command from Beowulf through the frenzied noise of horses and men. Halted, the troop listened to the cries for assistance and the terrified neighs until the screams of beasts and riders wrinkled the surface of the ground and were stopped by the sucking bog.

'Who were they?' Hrethric whispered to the man ahead of him.

'I do not know. But Geat or Scylding, what is the difference? We shall all follow. It has set its mark on our flesh.'

Wealhtheow had said, 'The marsh is perilous to those

who do not know the tracks and who more plausible than Unferth to recount the sad story?' Fear jerked Hrethric's body. On each side of him stretched the grasping ooze.

'Will the guide direct us off the path?' he breathed to the scop. 'He is Unferth's churl.'

'I have thought of that, but Unferth would not risk it. The lives of his own men might be forfeited.'

For a time the company did not move forward. They sat, a line of armed fighters, balanced upon a narrow rib of earth, peering into the vast grey where their companions had floundered, and heard the bubbles break among the reeds.

Then they were shuffling on again. They uttered no protest. The oppressive forest, the polar heath, the murderous bog, had left them listless and they followed dully, leaning against their horses' necks. But gradually they became aware of a movement which accompanied them, thin wisps which rolled at the horses' feet, and as these grew visible, the men knew that the darkness was lifting.

Before, they had travelled through vacant air, over ground which had sunk under their horses' tread; now, at every impress of the hesitant hooves, mist steamed out of the weedy pelt of the marsh, scurried up the animals' flanks, and writhed about the horsemen's heads. It felt for their faces; it drew damp tentacles across their cheeks; it coiled about their chests and wrapped round their arms. Yet the troop pushed on, seeing the reeds decrease and the mud thicken. Whilst mist spiralled out of every pore of the heaving marsh. Its breath hung and congealed in the grey air, and men moaned as its grease clung to their skins.

Then that was behind them. The company halted. The guide turned and pushed through them, hunched, running to escape, anxious to hide himself in the mists of the marsh.

And the host looked upon the region to which they had been led by the man who was Unferth's churl.

At first they could see little. Only by a paler grey above their heads did they assume that it was dawn. The sky bent over them; they followed its dim arc but found no definite line to assure them of its base. There was no horizon. It was as if they stood on the rim of the world. They were gazing into a void and nothing except the darker air at their feet told them it was floored. There were no trees, no hills, no steep peaks lifting into the empty sky. There was no thatch that might have netted the sullen light in a hint of gold. They watched the day slink cautiously from its mottled source and saw it seep unwelcomed into the land.

But, strangely obstinate in this country which did not seem subject to natural laws, the dull light persisted and revealed ground warped round puddles of glazed sludge and webbed with shallow cracks. It was a shapeless region, bare and barren; nothing green broke through its crust; not even a stone interrupted its grey expanse; no natural creature had ever trod its wastes. This heavy air had never parted at the sound of men's laughter, and the troop held their breath, afraid of rupturing the silence, and knowing that they were the first of their kind to venture alive beyond this edge.

Finally, at a signal from Beowulf, they stepped forward, following the huge spoors which printed the ashy dust. It lay like a scurf over the bald land and it did not scatter at their horses' tread or rise in the windless air. Under its pall the ground had stiffened to a brittle scab which splintered beneath the pacing hooves, and from the fissures a black slime oozed. It filled their nostrils with a stench of decay.

They saw that they journeyed through a land diseased, and as its foulness coursed through their heads and entered their lungs, they coughed, and fought desperately for more wholesome breath.

But there was none. For the region was infected, consigned to endless rot; a condition worse than death. Then, as the tracks ended at a leaden pool, to the vapours of the earth was added the smell of putrefying flesh.

Strewn round the lip of the pool, like undigested scraps vomited from its maw, half-chewed lumps of meat festered, discarded gristle yellowed, entrails were tangled among gnawed bones and, on the mould of the pool's sludge, lungs lay bloated. Sickened, retching, the men drew closer in an attempt to find comfort in living warmth, but surrounded by gobbets of the Scylding dead, none dared look into his companions' eyes. A word roused them and they lifted their gaze to where Beowulf pointed.

'We have reached our goal,' he said quietly.

It was less than they had expected yet consistent with the region, swelling like a tumour upon the scabrous earth. There were no gables, no chiselled pillars; roof and walls were one, sloping to a blunt head from the roughly circular base. The sides of caked sludge presented no facets to the slatey light; its squat form did not stretch up but clung to the rotting ground. Excreted out of the slime, it hunched upon the low earth, as repulsive as the creature which it housed.

Beowulf gave a brief order and two of the Geats cantered in a wide circle round the featureless hump.

'There is none, my lord. The sides are blank,' they reported back.

They could see no entrance to the monster's lair.

The company gathered and considered, looking over the flat land whose endless space was broken by nothing except the crouched mound and the expanse of sludge at their feet. Until the meaning of the thick pool came to them.

'It is the hole left by their digging,' Hrothulf said. 'They made their lair out of this sterile clay.'

'Scooped with their claws, sticking to their hands, kneaded and daubed over the waste to become a stunted chamber,' Angenga murmured.

'Without an entrance.'

'The tracks do not approach it. They stop here,' another observed. Then the rest understood.

'It will be a long tunnel. From this pool to the lair is at least fifty paces. It will run deep underground, starting at the bottom of the pool and coming up inside the lair.'

'Full of this vile stew.'

'Yes. Nevertheless I must swim it,' Beowulf said.

'No, my lord! That would be madness!' A Geat expressed the company's horror. 'It is a foul sump, a cesspool floating with ordure and putrid flesh. No beast would enter it. Our stallions rear at the very smell. It is not a place for a warrior, my lord.'

'That is irrelevant. I must reach the monster's dam. Lash spears together, plunge them in and find out the depth.' Looking over the pool he kept his face expressionless, concealing his disgust.

'I cannot allow you to undertake this, Beowulf,' the king said. 'Your companion's argument is just. This is no place for honourable combat. It defiles us. Already our armour is smirched with the spittle of the bog and tarnishes in the vapours of this loathsome region. When I accepted your offer to fight the she-monster, I did not imagine that she

148

was moated by this mire. This danger was not part of my agreement.'

'Nor mine, my lord.' Beowulf's tone was even. 'But there is no alternative.'

'Perhaps we can devise one.' A number of Geats, unwilling but forced to obey their leader's command, were sounding the pool's depth. 'It is not wise to confront the monster now, to invade her lair when you are weary and when the final path to it has been through a conduit of stifling slime. We will wait until night. We will circle this pool and fall upon her when she swims up for prey.'

'The fight is best confined within her chamber. I prefer to meet her alone. That is my resolve. No other life will be risked.'

'Beowulf, neither of us underestimates the nature of this fight. Few men imagined you would succeed against the first demon though the power of your body tempted us to hope. But that was a contest of strength, right against evil. This is the feud of blood.'

'Yes, my lord, and I have promised to end it, confronting the she-monster as your son. But if fate decrees that I shall meet my death in her fetid lair, I shall be satisfied. I leave my troop in your keeping and I ask you to be generous to them and see them embarked safely for our Geat land if I do not return.'

Hrothgar straightened and clamped his horse with his thighs. His white cloak was spotted with mud; fatigue had deepened the lines on his face, but his eyes were commanding as he regarded the younger man. 'We cannot alter what fate has ordained for us, Beowulf. But we do not rush to assist her,' he added with a wry smile. 'You shall not undertake this venture, my son. I do not permit it.'

149

He raised himself on his horse as if he would follow this command with an address to the whole company, and so he saw what a Geat was levering out of the pool and watched it curve up then oscillate in the leaden air. His body went rigid and he moaned.

Skewered on the point of the Geat's spear was the head of Aeschere. It was pasted with slime, the hair flat upon the scalp, the face smooth and eyeless as a mask. Tossed carelessly into the sludge, fished out by chance on the end of a probing spear, and now wagging and nodding grotesquely at its former companions, it reminded them of the reason for their journey, cautioned them, and talked to them of the frailty and transience of their flesh. Yet it had a strange dignity. Though abused, it was still the head of a man. Under the loathsome slime it was private, solemn, unconquerable.

'We will bury him with proper ceremony, Father,' Hrethric said.

Hrothgar nodded, his face bleak, and gestured to the Geat. The spear was lowered. As the head tilted, mud slid from the face and the mouth leered out at them, twisted in the agony of mortal pain. With a splitting cry, Hrothgar leapt from his horse, grasped the head in both hands, jerked it off the spear and cradled it against his chest. He stood with the slime of the ground bubbling over his feet, the hem of his mantle scraping the dung, the mire of the demon's pool plastering his hands, weeping at the anguish which was set for ever upon his friend's cold face and which would never loosen under his warm tears.

Afterwards, when they had lifted him back on his horse, when his sobs had diminished to whimpers, when by no coaxing could they persuade him to give up the head, they turned to consult together and found that their foremost warrior had gone.

His cloak lay in tidy folds by the side of the pool, and he had placed his helmet upon it so that the bright gold should be safe from the encroaching slime. Upon its crest the figure of the boar stood flexed in readiness for the attacking leap, and the gems in its eyes looked out across the pool towards the dun mound of the monster's lair.

# TWELVE

So the company waited. Their faces were weary, their bodies slack. Fixed on the pool, their eyes were empty of hope. This was no pause before battle when they felt exhilarated with courage and the strange thrill of fear. Their thoughts dragged through the mire, halted at the entrance to the monster's chamber, then frantically staggered back, and the men grew faint with suffocating dread. In this light which smouldered like cooling ore, they had no knowledge of time; there was no sun to tell the passage of the day. They were adrift on a land where no hours or seasons united them to the rhythms of the earth, and only by the sweat which welled from their pores and the nausea in their bowels were they assured that they still lived. They stayed close together, Geats and Scyldings, round the blank king, and no noise except his infant babbles disturbed the silence as he rocked the severed head in his arms.

'Is there nothing we can do for him?' Hrethric asked the scop.

'No, it is best to allow his grief a vent.'

'I wish we could find him a place to rest.'

That was impossible. They could not lay him upon the foul crust. Filth oozed from every crack made by their horses' hooves and no one had dismounted. Occasionally, to relieve his tired stallion, a man would ride away a little distance then return quickly to his companions. But two, Hrothulf and Unferth, kept apart watching the pool's

152

unrippled sludge and from time to time one would glance over his shoulder at the distracted king.

Observing them, Hrethric whispered, 'Do you think they plot to attack us? Like this, he would not be difficult to depose,' and drew his horse nearer to his father.

'There could not be a better opportunity,' Angenga replied. 'Many reasons could be given in the court for the king's death and the loss of faithful duguth. No one would venture here to recover the slain. How many of Unferth's men do you see?'

'Their number equals the rest.'

'At present the feud binds them to Hrothgar. See how they remain by his side. But who can predict how men will act in extremity? This land is evil, breeding nothing but death.'

Loud voices covered his last words. Two men were arguing, their faces flushed by the sunless heat. There was a brief scuffle across their horses, a sharp challenge, and they galloped off, scattering clods in a wide path round the pool. A few cheers greeted the first to return and the loser, with horse limping, did not rejoin the rest. Obliged to examine his horse, he stood in the murk and when he had grown tired of cursing his competitor, he stayed where he was, frowning and looking sidelong at Hrothulf and his friend.

'So . . .' the scop murmured.

'Hrothulf has lost credit with them for not offering himself when my mother begged but I do not think that will last. Unferth intimidates them,' the young man observed in a low voice. 'It is more important that my cousin learnt the queen's true feelings. You saw his face then?'

'Yes. He no longer believes that she would support his claim. There is, perhaps, greater danger to you than to your father. He may make an attack on your life.'

'Then I shall defend it. Till the flesh is hacked from my bones.'

'I do not doubt it; and I shall stand with you. Did we not once share your sacrificial pig?' He smiled, remembering. 'But age has blunted my skill in the fight. It would be better to hope for the thing that would prevent Hrothulf: the Geat's successful return.'

The knowledge of Beowulf's danger came back to him. Hrethric looked towards the faceless chamber; his vision, blurred and unfocused, gave him two bodies struggling. One whiskery, with hanging dugs, felled the other with a blow of a swinging arm; bones snapped between black fangs and a head oiled with sludge rolled at his feet. His father whimpered and his son reached down, lifted the head that was Aeschere's and replaced it carefully in the king's groping hands.

Hrethric's wounds throbbed. Around him, the men fretted. The heat had increased. Sweat dried as it was drawn from their skin, and the slime that had oozed was stiffening again under the horses' feet. Caught by a stallion's tail, a man swore and threatened the rider. The Scylding who had lost the race now lolled by Unferth. A number of the counsellor's supporters, on the pretext of examining the pool, had moved to his side, and the Geat who had been Hondscio's friend was scowling at Hrethric and muttering to his neighbour. The prince looked at his father. Whatever happened, his son must lead them now. He ran his fingers over the hilt of Aeschere's sword and regarded the company, counting those on whom he could rely.

'We will offer a sacrifice to the deity,' he said quietly to Angenga. 'We will shackle a horse and lay it before a shield, armour of the Scyldings, men of the shield; and I will spear the horse in the chest. If Beowulf still lives, the sacrifice may persuade the deity to send him back unharmed. Or, if he is already dead, the blood of a war stallion may coax her to look favourably upon me and to cripple any hand that may be raised against my life.'

'Hush; not yet. I, too, have been thinking. There may be another way.' Turning slightly in his saddle, so that in the most natural manner he was visible to all the men, he continued, 'There are many deities, my lord. I have heard of many in my travels. To them, men sacrifice beasts; to them, priests offer the blood of fellow men; to them have been given the chosen ones noosed with ceremonial cords. Here, among the tribes of these islands, men and women have been sacrificed and their bodies given back to our earth mother in the hope that she would bless the land with the riches of fruit and crops. But I have heard of another deity who demanded a sacrifice different from these.'

For a moment the creases under his eyes were pinched as he stared intensely at Hrethric and the prince knew that the scop was intending something besides the telling of a new story. He had modulated his voice so that his words reached every man in the company, but as yet he gave no sign that he knew his speech was overheard.

'It was a woman who told me. She had been captured after a battle, one of many women our warriors took after they had killed their men and laid waste their homes. She was a pretty creature, with a vixen's spirit.' Responding at last to the stir of interest, he looked round with a feigned surprise, then as if confiding, 'Those tribes that possessed the new Anglia before our hosts conquered are fierce and bloody. Their women are wild and not easily subdued. This one I tell you of had a tongue like a whip's lash, teeth as sharp as daggers' points, and nails that could rake your flesh into bleeding furrows. I still bear their scars upon me.' Fumbling under his cloak, he stroked his chest ruefully, and contrived to blush at their laughter. He had tickled their lewdness; now he could play them as he wished.

'Oh, you may laugh. But I tell you those women fought in the chamber as their men did in the field, furiously, remorselessly. They accompanied their men into battle; they tell stories of a queen who long ago led her warriors against a Roman host. But my woman recounted other stories, during the moments when she was nearly tamed.'

The scop lowered his voice, forcing the company to step closer. 'She was young, that woman, mocking my age, and her youth and her stories were better weapons than her nails. She would squat on my furs, clinging to the rags she would not let me replace, and scoff at my misery – my misery at the knowledge that some day the earth, its beauty that has sustained me, and the fellowship of our kind, will recede from my grasp. She, a captive, mocked, and she taunted me with the promise of her deity whom she called God. His story had come to the shores of her tribe, brought by men from a land where the sun rides a cloudless sky and no frosts kill the ripening fruit on the stem. This God was gentle and treated kindly those who relinquished other deities to worship his name, and he promised his followers that they would live again after their death.

'No, like you, I could not believe it. I could not believe in a benevolent deity. While frost gripped my bones; while the storms and snow of those winters lashed the land and ice split the earth under my tread, I could not believe that there could be a deity who would fold me to his bosom.

The deity I know is pitiless; she promises nothing. Yet the stories of her God linger; they stay in the mind, and the one that she told most often is the strangest of all.'

There was no longer any need for Angenga to employ the tricks of a performer. The heat was forgotten; the stench was wafted from their nostrils; the barren land round them dropped from their sight as they watched his face.

'I have said her deity was gentle. He demanded her praise and her prayers. She would speak to him in the darkness as if he were a man sharing her bed, while I wept that the words were not uttered to me. He did not demand sacrifice, though she said his worshippers would give their lives to prove the truth of his story. She never offered him any bird or beast, because, she said, a sacrifice had been made.

'She told me that her deity had appeared on this earth, in the warmer region from where the priest came. He had come as a man and called himself the son of this God. Many of her stories were about this son, and when his time came to die, he let men fasten him to a tree. It took him three days to die, hanging there under the sun. That was his sacrifice. This deity, who was the son of her God, sacrificed himself to his father. Do you understand me? He did not sacrifice a beast, or a priest, but *himself*. And he did this, she said, for men on this earth. He did this, she said, so that her deity would assuage his anger, so that men should have life after death. When they had buried him, his body rose up and was seen to walk in the light of day, and those that saw him believed that there was a life beyond the grave. I wish I could believe that,' Angenga said, looking at the silent mound. 'I wish I could believe that a man who had sacrificed himself for his kind could rise out of his mound and feast again with his companions.'

157

His words were an epitaph to the Geat warrior. No one disputed them. They had waited long. No man among them could deceive himself that Beowulf still lived. Gazing over the turgid pool, each one mourned.

'It is a good story, Scop,' a thane said.

'Yes, and worthy to be put into song. I shall remember it when I sing of the Geat.'

Their wait was over but they did not stir. Beowulf had led them there and without him all impulse to action was removed. Sluggishly their minds turned to the she-monster. They would become her prey, but grief and the rigours of the journey made them apathetic and like creatures wearied by the hunt they surrendered themselves to the devouring teeth. Yet, even as he wept, Hrethric noticed that his cousin and Unferth were whispering together and the threat which lurked within the humped chamber was replaced by the menace of their swords.

'We must go,' he urged Angenga. 'Here, a fight has ground and however well we combat, it is a chance matter who wins. On the path through the marsh it is less easy for them to form up to attack and I will keep the loyal duguth in the rear so that no surprise is possible.'

Roused from private grieving, Angenga absorbed his words. 'So you take command, my prince?'

'My father is too feeble now. I act for him.'

'I praise your decision, but what about Hrothulf? He has ruled with your father many winters.'

'If he questions me outright, I shall challenge him to single combat.'

The scop smiled. 'You are headstrong, Hrethric. He is an experienced warrior. I doubt if your skill equals your courage. I cannot prevent you, but please, before you assume the authority of the king, let an exiled traveller finish his story,' and without pausing for the other to agree, he turned back to the men.

'So, like other deities, the deity of my woman received a sacrifice, and the man who was that sacrifice said that he was the deity's son,' the scop continued as if musing aloud and the bowed heads of the company were raised to him. There was relief in the distraction afforded by a bard.

'I have heard no similar tale in my travels, but I know, as you do, many warriors who gave their lives for their lord. I would argue that with my woman, demanding, "Why was his courage greater than the courage of a man who gives his life for his lord? That warrior does not pretend to provide his lord with a life after death – he dies that his lord may continue to live on this earth. What makes the sacrifice of your deity so important?" Forgive me, my friends; I shout as I did to her. The memory of her obstinacy can send a man crazed.' Momentarily they grinned, united with him as they recalled the stubbornness of women.

'She was like a rock based on the floor of the sea; nothing could move her. She said that his sacrifice had been to placate her God, to turn his anger from the wickedness of men. All men were wicked because once one man had eaten a magic fruit which her God denied him. I paid no heed to such a tale, but other things she said about our wickedness, which she called sin, these other things had more sense.

'I would listen to her through the long night and her voice would people the darkness with shapes I knew and I would sweat at her words, as you would have sweated, my friends. Understand me, there was nothing new in her descriptions; at first it was their familiarity that persuaded me that in one thing her deity spoke truth. We know of misshapen beasts, of giants, of spirits that lie in wait under the hill, of hostile creatures of the deep, of demons spewed out of the rocks' fissures, of monsters that tread the wastes.' He paused a moment as the men rustled fearfully. 'But it was not fear of their presence which made me sweat in the darkness, my friends. It was terror. Terror, when she told me the origin of these unnatural creatures. Terror, because I knew that what she said was true; because I knew that there is no greater wickedness possible than that which had caused their evil to multiply upon this lovely earth.'

His voice was raised. It commanded the whole company. Round him, the warriors were fixed and staring; further off, Unferth, Hrothulf and their followers were still; and Hrethric observed that for the first time the king had raised his eyes from Aeschere's head. The scop's face was intense and he spoke with passion. Whatever role he had played was forgotten now.

'There in my chamber in the new Anglia, there in my sweating night, I heard her voice telling me that all these evil ones, all the evil things which set their hideous prints upon the face of our earth, they are the spawn of spawn, the descendants of one man who lived long ago. He was called Cain. Though tricked out like a man he had a spirit ugly with wickedness. His evil lives on in the hearts of his monstrous children, and the thing he did is performed again and again by creatures who have the bodies of men but the same evil hearts as lie in these unnatural beasts. His act is not unknown to you. It is one you have witnessed. Cain's act went unavenged, as the one known to you is unavenged. Because of that wickedness, evil stalks freely among you, and men who believe themselves to be the sons of deities, and warriors whose selflessness and courage is beyond our valuation continue to sacrifice themselves to save us. The act and the sacrifice are repeated. My friends, you have already guessed the evil that Cain committed. He took his brother and slew him before the face of his lord.'

Exhausted, the scop slumped against his horse's neck. For a moment whose length it was impossible to measure, the men were motionless, dumb with shock. Then suddenly one cried out and all eyes followed the direction of his stare. The men by the pool started.

'Stay where you are!' Unferth hissed and stared back at the accusing men.

His face was white but controlled. 'A pretty story of country superstitions, swollen with rhetoric,' he pronounced loudly across the ground. 'It has frightened the timorous and angered me, which I am sure was not what you purposed, Scop. However, the entertainment is now over. There is business to settle.'

He glanced quickly at Hrothulf, then at the men by their side, among whom was the Geat who had been Hondscio's friend. Stunned by Angenga's denunciation, they looked back appalled but the habit of deference to him kept them where they were. His cruel authority cowed them into obedience. Not knowing what words he intended, Hrethric took a breath, but speech was prevented as the Geat by Unferth uttered a loud shriek.

Seeping through fistulas in the pool's sludge, a skinny foam was creeping across the surface. As the light bubbles broke, their airy membranes cohered to a thin brown which gradually spread as from a leaking wound over the stagnant grey. The stain grew; it covered the pool, and the men knew they looked upon flowing blood.

It confirmed what they were already sure of, but the sight of his blood was terrible to them; it thrust the details of his combat upon them and, precisely, each one imagined his death.

'It is all that remains,' the Geat by the pool moaned. Dismounted, he bent down and scooped up blood in his hands.

'Who expected anything more?' Unferth demanded sharply. 'He presumed to interfere in a Scylding feud.' It was a thoughtless retort born of jealousy, carelessly thrown out as he stepped forward with Hrothulf to challenge the king. And he paid a high price for it.

For the Geat shouted and sprang across his path. 'Murderer!' he yelled and threw the blood in Unferth's face.

Immediately there was an uproar. Men were shouting. Mud was crunching under hooves. Swords clanged against shields. Horses neighed as crossed spears scratched their necks. Until the struggling mass resolved. Loyal duguth circled Hrothgar; others stood in a loose unwilling group beside Hrothulf, and the troop of Geats was formed behind their new leader. Facing them, Unferth sat his horse. He held himself straight and looked back at them with contempt.

'He has sacrificed his life and you mocked him,' the Geat said with slow emphasis.

'If your words are meant as a challenge,' Unferth answered, his lips narrowing, 'then I accept it and we will fight it out.' Poised high on his horse, he turned his head with no undignified haste and made a slight, elegant gesture towards his men.

The rest waited. Heat smoked from the hollow sky; the

162

blood set at the sludge's edge; the rotting flesh baked and split; the monster's chamber crouched on the festering ground. The stench of corruption filled their nostrils while they looked at Unferth and watched the blood of Beowulf and the pus from Grendel's pool mingle and slide as from an ulcer down Unferth's cheeks. Scyldings and Geats together let out a low growl.

At last one of his men answered the signal. 'I will not fight for you. You slew a brother. I always knew that, but your tongue is plausible and charmed me to forget. I am thankful that I have done nothing dishonourable, though my thoughts give me shame.' He moved away, along the margin of the sludge, and gradually one by one his companions followed.

Unferth watched them go. 'Then I will fight alone. I do not stoop to beg the assistance of cowards.' Once more, he regarded the Geats and though his gaze was haughty no one could deny his courage. He was again the warrior whose fearlessness had strengthened Hrothgar's host in former times; and at this last he showed himself selfless, remaining loyal to his friend, for he did not jeopardize Hrothulf's position by claiming his support.

'I am ready,' and lowered his spear.

'It shall be a single combat,' the Geat answered and gestured to his company to hold back.

'Who gives the word?' the counsellor demanded.

'There shall be no word,' a frail voice answered and, pushing through the cordon around him, Hrothgar advanced slowly to the head of the Geat troop. His face was grey; the anguished head was still clutched to his breast; his horse's patience, not his own skill held him to the saddle, and he regarded them all with the irritation of a man dragged from meditation to petty duty.

Almost petulantly, he continued, 'No man fights without the permission of the king. What folly is it that prompts combat between you while the she-monster still breathes in her lair? I have listened to the stories; I have heard your quarrels; they have prodded through my grief for Aeschere and scraped the tender quick of my guilt. No man, either Geat or Scylding, shall stand against Unferth. He is my burden. I, and I alone, allowed his fratricide to go unpunished. Perhaps it was my weakness that encouraged other evil to molest me and my people, I do not know, but the scop's story warns us. Many brave ones are sacrificed; two I loved more than myself are forever gone from me; before this day ends we may all be carrion. But one deed I will perform. If it is my last, I shall give thanks as the blood is sucked from my veins that I requited a wrong that has soiled the name of a Scylding king.

'You, Unferth, I banish. Your horse and armour take with you, this jewel from my finger and golden band from my wrist. To the tribes of the Scyldings, to those on the islands that girdle our shores, you are now an alien; it is unlawful to harbour you. You must wander friendless over the wide regions of the earth and must suffer the penalty for your wickedness until the end of your days.'

Hrothgar stepped forward and handed the ring and the armlet to the man who had once been his counsellor. The assembly stood, shocked and mute. This punishment was worse than death in battle; even death under the claws of the she-monster was preferable to this disgrace.

Unferth bowed as he received the king's last gifts. His lips quivered but he did not speak. No appeal was possible and he did not attempt one; neither did he utter any farewell but, as his eyes swept over the company, they lingered for a moment upon Hrothulf. Then he drew himself straight, kicked his stallion, and cantered out of their midst.

The host watched as he rode across the waste alone, watched him grow smaller until horse and rider merged into the dun ground, then Hrothgar turned to his son. 'We will go back now. See to it, Hrethric,' and paced his horse to the pool where he sat looking down at the caked blood.

Hrethric blushed at his father's words and the knowledge that every man in the company had turned to him. By this modest gesture the king had delegated his authority, and his heir was accepted. The men crowded round him, waiting for him to speak, and the Scyldings who had remained loyal to Hrothgar and those who had supported his cousin Hrothulf, together gave him their trust. Only Hrothulf kept apart, stroking his horse's neck and gazing at the crescent prints brimming with slime which were the last tracks of his friend.

'Speed is essential,' Hrethric heard himself say. 'We must cross the marsh before dusk. Two of the Geats carry Beowulf's helmet and mantle. I will lead his horse. Keep close.' His eyes swept round them until they found the Geat who was Hondscio's friend and who had challenged Unferth. 'You, Geat warrior, I ask you to lead us over this land, just as your lord did,' and saw the man's gratitude. Past accusations were irrelevant now. 'The king and my cousin will ride after the Geats, then the rest of the Scyldings. But when this region ends, stop and wait for me. I shall go first over the marsh.'

They nodded and bowed, then swerved away, walking their horses as quickly as possible through the cracking mud. One brought Beowulf's horse to Hrethric and, as the host

moved off, he said to the scop, 'He made little use of this.'
He stroked the war saddle.'Yesterday I was displeased at my
father's giving it. I did not imagine that the first time he
rode it would be to his death.'

'No.'

'I am too tired now to think of the monster's dam –
whether she will attack us in the future instead of her son
– but Unferth is banished. There is comfort in that. I cannot
believe that Hrothulf's power is totally destroyed or his
tongue silenced, but he has lost his chief ally. Things will be
better in the Scylding court, Angenga, and I have you to
thank for that.'

'That is something.'

'Is it not everything? Your story reminded Unferth's men
of what he is. It showed them their own conduct. As a
result our court is rid of a disgrace, of a murderer who
schemed continually against his king.'

'You offer me a justification. My mind can accept it, but
not my heart.'

'A justification? Is this another riddle?'

'No, it is not a riddle.' The man's voice was sombre.
Miserably he regarded the print at his feet. 'Do you not
understand? I told a story, and because of that a man is
exiled.'

'His exile was deserved.'

'No doubt, but I was the cause. He is banished and I
used my talent for that purpose. I, a poet, have abused my
craft.'

'Have you not said that a poet reveals men to themselves,
that he offers them knowledge?'

'That is a bitter reminder, Hrethric. It is true; but I
am responsible for another's pain and henceforth in my

wanderings I shall be accompanied by the shade of another exile. My shoulders will stoop with his friendless burden and my feet will drag with his lonely ache.'

'Perhaps when you sing of him you will find something to relieve him. Though corrupt, he was loyal to my cousin.' Hrethric was surprised at his suggestion. It contradicted his previous notions of men. What had his mother said about Hrothulf? 'A man capable of such affection must have within him some good.'

'You are a good teacher,' Angenga said.

The last Scylding had left the pool. The column of horsemen was the only thing that moved upon the level waste. But as they turned to follow, Hrethric and the scop saw the mire shift. Folds slid like slow ripples towards the edge and the centre bulged.

'It is she,' Hrethric gasped, and simultaneously he and Angenga drew their swords.

The swelling increased; it advanced towards them, lifted to a peak as the swimmer found footing and began to wade, until suddenly the stiff tent of sludge fell back and the head and shoulders of a man broke through the pool's skin.

Speechless, they watched him come, slowly, pushing at the encumbering stew, then his feet were on the brittle crust of the ground. His body was slicked with slime and he stood before them, exuding the pool's stench.

'It is you!' was all Hrethric could whisper.

Beowulf made no answer but his head jerked towards the low mound.

'You have killed the dam?' Angenga said.

Again the head jerked and the hands came up. They were rigid, bent like claws, as if set for ever in a strangling grasp.

'Are you wounded?'

167

He did not reply but the mire was peeling off his chest and they could see the rings of his corslet distorted, and the iron scored by a blade.

'She had a dagger?'

In response, Beowulf dragged something from his belt. They saw a hilt of gnawed bone, a broad blade with toothed edge, then it was flung into the air and penetrated the circle of sludge.

'We assumed you were dead. We saw the blood.'

They were alarmed by his silence. Praise, gladness, any movement to wipe off the filth was halted before the man's blank stare.

At last Angenga said, 'We must go, Beowulf. Let us help you to your horse.'

He stood dumbly while they brought the horse to his side but he made no attempt to mount. Hrethric and the scop struggled together but by no effort could they raise them.

'Come, straddle your horse. We wait for you, Beowulf. The host is already far ahead and Hrethric is to lead us across the marsh,' Angenga persuaded. 'It is all over, my lord. You have done what you promised. She is dead, and her lair is behind you.'

At which, Beowulf glanced quickly towards the grey mound. A spasm passed through his body. He looked at his two companions as if seeing them for the first time. The mask of slime on his face split and a thin spittle oozed from his mouth. Disregarding it, abandoned to private torment, Beowulf moaned and gradually through his strange keening they distinguished words.

'I was wombed with her! We were wombed together in that darkness, both of us reeking with the dung of that pool, stuck together with it, her breath on my mouth, her greasy thighs stroking my belly, her sour dugs pressed upon my chest. She would not loosen. I could not break her embrace. That was her revenge!'

His speech was stopped by shudders, then continued. 'And I felt my mind crumbling, as if it were a tangible thing that could be grasped and crushed even as I breathed; and for a space I surrendered to her foulness.'

He turned his face from them and laid his head upon the saddle that was the gift of the Scylding king. His shoulders lifted and fell; his body rocked, and through his wrenched weeping they heard him whimper, 'I was afraid. My spirit bowed to hers. Locked in her arms I was no longer a Geat warrior.'

He lifted his head and stared up at the two men. 'You must know this, my prince Hrethric, and you, Scop. For a space she made me her creature, and I was afraid. I was afraid, I tell you. I was afraid of what I had become.'

Appalled, they stared back at him. They could find no words to ease his self-disgust. But behind them the sludge had settled. It would never open again; and in the cooling heat of the afternoon the vapours of decay were withdrawing into the ground's fissures.

'But you killed her, Beowulf,' Hrethric said.

'Yes, when my spirit returned and she drew her dagger upon me.' So he dismissed his victory. To him it was nothing, compared with hers.

'We must live with our frailties, Beowulf,' Angenga said gently. 'Though I have never regarded fear as a weakness. Because, through fear, a man will often learn his true strength.'

They stood together, three men and their stallions, the

only breathing things on that dead earth, and they watched their shadows grow until they touched the brown stain which was Grendel's blood.

'It was his blood you saw,' Beowulf said. 'His body was there in the chamber. I groped until I found the head and severed it, so that his spirit should not return to haunt your hall.'

Then he climbed upon his horse and the three men turned their backs on the still pool and the hunched mound. Weary, but for this time at peace, they set their faces towards the sucking bog, the heath and the forest. Beyond which lay the golden beauty of Heorot.

## *AUTHOR'S NOTE*

As will be clear to readers familiar with the poem *Beowulf*, this novel is not a translation. Sections unrelated to the plot have been omitted and several additions made, notably the exile Angenga as a witness and subsequent recorder. Hrethric is given a central place and Unferth a less admirable one. Hints in the poem of Hrothulf's ambitions, which are supported by the historical probability of his final seizure of the throne, have been developed within the events of my narrative.